100 Reasons to Celebrate

We invite you to join us in celebrating
Mills & Boon's centenary. Gerald Mills and
Charles Boon founded Mills & Boon Limited
in 1908 and opened offices in London's Covent
Garden. Since then, Mills & Boon has become
a hallmark for romantic fiction, recognised
around the world.

We're proud of our 100 years of publishing
excellence, which wouldn't have been achieved
without the loyalty and enthusiasm of our
authors and readers.

Thank you!

Each month throughout the year there will
be something new and exciting to mark the
centenary, so watch for your favourite authors,
captivating new stories, special limited
edition collections…and more!

Dear Reader

The two Edwardian gentlemen who set up a publishing firm under their names wouldn't have known that in a century's time their fledgling business would be known all over the world for its expertise in publishing romances. I'm sure they'd have been delighted to know that their publishing empire would be not only flourishing but famous in the twenty-first century.

It's a great pleasure to be part of that history and one of the Mills & Boon team of authors, publishing professionals and readers. Like every other Mills & Boon author I've met, I started off as a reader, loving the books and eagerly looking forward to each month's ration. I still do. Where else can I get carried away to a world where love flourishes in spite of almost insurmountable problems and I'm guaranteed a happy ending?

HIS MAJESTY'S MISTRESS is the first of two books about twin sisters; this one tells of Giselle, the oldest— by half an hour—and will be followed by Leola's story. I do hope you enjoy them.

My gratitude and very best wishes to the hard-working staff at Mills & Boon in this centenary year, to the writers who please us month after month, and to all those loyal readers who are the foundation of the success of the past hundred years.

Robyn Donald

HIS MAJESTY'S MISTRESS

BY
ROBYN DONALD

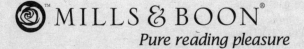

MILLS & BOON

Pure reading pleasure

All the characters in this book have no existence outside the imagination of the author, and have no relation whatsoever to anyone bearing the same name or names. They are not even distantly inspired by any individual known or unknown to the author, and all the incidents are pure invention.

First published in Great Britain 2008
Harlequin Mills & Boon Limited,
Eton House, 18-24 Paradise Road, Richmond, Surrey TW9 1SR

© Robyn Donald 2008

ISBN: 978 0 263 86412 0

Set in Times Roman 10½ on 12¼ pt
01-0308-49400

Printed and bound in Spain
by Litografia Rosés, S.A., Barcelona

Robyn Donald has always lived in Northland in New Zealand, initially on her father's stud dairy farm at Warkworth, then in the Bay of Islands, an area of great natural beauty, where she lives today with her husband and an ebullient and mostly Labrador dog. She resigned her teaching position when she found she enjoyed writing romances more, and now spends any time not writing in reading, gardening, travelling, and writing letters to keep up with her two adult children and her friends.

Recent titles by the same author:

VIRGIN BOUGHT AND PAID FOR
THE PRINCE'S CONVENIENT BRIDE

CHAPTER ONE

ALMOST the last thing Maura said at Auckland airport was, 'Now enjoy yourself!'

Giselle Foster smiled. 'Of course I will.'

Her godmother gently urged her towards the departure gate. 'When you come back I want to see clear eyes—without the shadows underneath—and a spring in your step. And some colour in your cheeks. You've worked far too hard for far too long, and that flu turning to pneumonia was a warning.'

'You know I've always been lily-white. Leola's the twin with golden skin and pink cheeks! And someone has to keep Parirua going,' Giselle said defensively, checking her travel documents.

The older woman looked at her with too much perception. 'Just because it's been in your family for generations doesn't mean you're obliged to make it your life's work.'

'I love it,' Giselle said.

Maura sighed. 'I know, I know. Too much—but don't let me start on that. Just try to forget about the station and the cattle and the farm workers and the mortgage for the next fortnight.'

If only it were that easy! But Giselle nodded. 'OK.'

'You'll probably find Coconut Bay too noisy and brash for you at first, so ease yourself into things. Have fun. Go a little wild—flirt lots, and laugh more.' She smiled and kissed Giselle's cheek, then gave her a little push, adding sternly, 'And make sure you rest every afternoon. I want to see some colour in your cheeks when you come back.'

Giselle hugged her. 'Thank you so much for not only organising this holiday, but paying for it. I promise to enjoy every second.'

But after only three of the fourteen days she was to spend on the tropical island of Fala'isi, Giselle was ready to slink back to New Zealand. Although it was exquisitely beautiful, and the resort lived up to its reputation for non-stop activity, most of it was wasted on her. The universal high spirits seemed tiresome, even a little desperate; drinking cocktails in a crowd held no allure to her, and she didn't know how—or even want—to embark on a holiday flirtation.

And lying on the beach to burnish a tan wasn't an option; her pale skin needed careful nurturing, so she had to sprint for shelter after each swim.

Also, it was impossible to avoid people unless she stayed in her room. Everyone was so openly friendly, it made her feel ungrateful and sullen to long for solitude and quiet.

Which was why she had just hauled one of the resort's small, garish sailing dinghies across the skirt of dazzling sand that surrounded a tiny island, a green bead on the edge of the reef. She took a deep breath once again, grateful to the high school teacher who'd given his time after school to teach an enthusiastic group the rudiments of small boat sailing.

All was peace and calm and blissful silence except for the faint rustling of the palm leaves in the warm wind. Even the long combers that normally smashed noisily against the reef had transmuted into wavelets purring against the coral. No footstep marred the pristine beach; it promised serenity and splendid isolation. Giselle's gaze drifted further, across a lagoon as impossibly blue as the sky. Not a sail in sight.

Sighing happily, she carried her picnic hamper through the palms into the shade beneath several sprawling trees, their leafy lower branches hiding her from view.

That thought made her laugh out loud. Nobody was going to stroll by. 'Perfect,' she breathed—secluded, with delightful glimpses of the open sea through the foliage.

She spread out her towel, loosened the sarong that covered her bikini and took her book from her bag. Beneath it was a digital camera, an extra gift from Maura.

Giselle spent some time taking snaps of the huge sweep of ocean that reached all the way to Tahiti, its immensity emphasised by a solitary yacht making its way up the coast.

Then she sank down onto the towel and opened her book. The only reading material in the resort shop seemed to be magazines that detailed the supposed romantic affairs of the jet set. Giselle was as interested as anyone in the lives of famous people, but an uninterrupted diet of it soon palled. Fortunately the resort also had a small library, and there she'd discovered the most recent book of one of her favourite authors. Time to read was a rare, highly prized luxury.

She stretched out to lose herself in a fantasy world.

Some time later she woke with a start, realising dimly that she'd been hearing voices in her sleep, a light woman's voice, and one belonging to a man.

She couldn't make out any words, but something made her hold her breath as she eased up to peer through the tangle of foliage separating her from the beach. The first thing she saw was a yacht anchored just inside the passage through the reef, a long, sleek obviously expensive thing with such beautiful lines it made her heart sing.

Two people were on the beach only a few metres from her refuge—a tanned, powerfully built man in a loose shirt and swimming shorts, and a woman wearing a white bikini that displayed slightly more than was necessary of her considerable assets. Her back was presented to the man who was smoothing sunscreen on it, a process she was enjoying enormously if her sensuous little stretches and murmurs were any indication.

An odd shiver ran down Giselle's spine. She suspected that she too would be purring like a kitten under those expert caresses.

He was facing Giselle, black head bent slightly while he said something, the sun on his face highlighting arrogant angles of his features.

An odd twist of sensation in the depths of her stomach startled Giselle. She swallowed to ease her dry throat. Big, sleekly muscled, he was a bronzed image of masculine power as he loomed protectively over the woman.

As she watched he laughed and said something to the woman, who tossed a glance that sizzled with invitation over her shoulder. Then she gave another voluptuous wriggle and leaned back against him.

He went very still, before getting to his feet in a single fluid movement, looking up the beach as he did so.

Giselle ducked down, because she had a horrid suspicion they were going to make love. Or perhaps had just made love. Whatever, she didn't want to be a spectator. She tried to shimmy backwards through the tangle of greenery, heart jumping when a dry stick cracked beneath her. Her gaze flew to the man on the beach.

He stood immobile for several seconds, his dark face intent, before turning back to the woman.

Breathing again, Giselle frowned as she scanned the woman's pouting face. She looked vaguely familiar, even while she was giving her companion what Giselle's god-mother, who enjoyed ancient slang, would have called a very come-hither look. Instead of responding to the open invitation the man made another comment, and after a shrug she too got up.

He bent to pick up a couple of bright cloths from the sand, then turned, his gaze once more searching the thick growth that hid the interior of the island.

Heart thudding so noisily in her chest she was afraid they might be able to hear it, Giselle froze again, hastily clamping her eyes shut to hide the shame of peeping.

He couldn't have known she was there. Although the crack of the stick had been loud to her, surely the noise couldn't have travelled that far?

He'd probably realised that an exposed beach was no place to make love. Much better to go back to that lovely yacht and have some privacy.

A little wistfully, Giselle let her lashes drift up and watched them walk out of sight. Her life meant she had no time and almost no desire to go out. But sometimes she dreamed of meeting someone…

Not, she thought sensibly, a man like that. His over-whelming male presence might have taken her breath away, but men like him didn't come along often, and they certainly weren't interested in women who worked as farm la-bourers. They could have anyone they wanted—beautiful, expensive women like the ones who graced the magazines in the resort shop.

A few minutes later she heard the distant buzz of a

motor, and watched a small speedboat appear from the yacht and head purposefully for the islet.

Who were they?

'Rich people,' she said dismissively. Yachts like that one came expensive.

And they'd both had that air of complete confidence, of a self-assurance so deep nothing could ruffle it.

The rich were different, and for a moment she envied them. Smiling with irony, she lifted her camera to take a photograph of the yacht as the sails were being raised.

'No, you don't. Give me that.' The voice came from just behind her, coldly commanding, and as she whirled the camera was wrenched from her hands.

Shocked into a gasp, she looked up into eyes of an astonishing clarity and colour; the deep, dark blue of the sky at midnight, they were hard and angry, set in a face even more strikingly handsome than she'd realised.

He towered above her, wide shoulders blocking out the sunlight. And although he wore a shirt, there was entirely too much rich bronze skin on view. It did very strange things to her bones.

If he touched her, she thought feverishly, she might burn like a torch.

Words stumbled from her tongue. 'Give me that!'

'No.' Before she could stop him he flicked through the stored photographs.

Outraged, she stammered, 'What the hell do you think you're doing?'

'Just checking,' he said briefly, and put the camera into the pocket of his shirt.

A faint intonation to his words made her suspect that English wasn't his first language. Although sexuality smoked off him like a haze, he kept his gaze fixed on her face; no surreptitious glances at her breasts in her bikini top, or inspection of her long legs.

Stung, Giselle blurted, 'You have no right—I didn't take any photographs of you.' And then stumbled into scarlet-cheeked silence, because she'd just made it obvious that she'd been watching.

His eyes narrowed into icy slivers. 'Who are you? Where do you come from? What do you want?'

The questions hammered at her like bullets. She drew in a deep breath and replied sturdily, 'I'm a guest at the Coconut Bay resort and I have just as much right to be here as you do.'

'Motukai—this island—is privately owned,' he said between his teeth. 'I don't believe any of the workers at the resort would have agreed to let you come here.'

Her skin burned even hotter. 'No one said not to.'

'Did you tell them you planned to sail here?'

'Well—no,' she admitted honestly. She'd intended to sail around a headland to a smaller, less crowded beach, but halfway across the lagoon she'd noticed the island and changed her mind. She added with spirit, 'If you want people to stay away you should scatter the island with No Trespassing signs.'

'It isn't needed,' he told her with breathtaking arrogance. 'Everyone knows to keep off it. Why did you take photos of the yacht?'

'It looks so lovely,' she said quietly, her fear subsiding a little.

One black brow lifted. 'White yacht on a turquoise lagoon, palm trees, the sound of the rollers breaking on the reef—all the tropical clichés,' he agreed with irony. Then, abruptly changing his tone, he asked, 'Would you like to go on board and have a look around?'

Stunned, she was almost tempted, but shook her head. 'No, thanks. I don't know you, and your attitude doesn't exactly fill me with confidence.'

A swift smile set her heart beating madly again. It was pure dynamite—intimate, amused, and challenging in a way that set off alarm bells. Giselle's stomach muscles clenched, and heat churned through her. She knew what it was, of course. Inexperienced she might be when it came to men, but she was woman enough to recognise physical attraction when it hit her in the solar plexus—and other vulnerable parts of her body.

Face it, she thought grimly. It had to happen eventually. So get over it. He probably does that to every woman he meets.

He knew he was gorgeous; he had the bone-deep confidence of someone with a charmed life.

'Touché,' he drawled. 'I'll help you get your stuff back to the sailing dinghy.'

In other words he was going to see her off. Stiff-backed, Giselle said coolly, 'You don't need to bother—I got them here, I'll take them back.'

But he ignored her, stooping to pick up her rug and hamper and carrying them through the dark shade of the trees. Out on the sand, Giselle stopped, frowning. Her little craft had been hauled into the water and was bobbing behind a small motorboat—not, she realised, the one that had come from the yacht to pick them up. There was no sign of the woman.

'I can sail back,' she said, stiff with unease.

He shrugged. 'It's easy enough sailing this way with the wind behind you,' he said lightly, 'but you'd have to tack back.'

'I know.' Patronising jerk! 'I've done quite a bit of sailing.'

He gave her a considering look calculated to set her teeth on edge. This man knew exactly the effect he wanted to have, and achieved it effortlessly.

'You're a New Zealander, aren't you?' he said.

'What's that got to do with anything?'

'You can stop bristling. Most New Zealanders seem to have an affinity for the sea.'

A satirical undertone set her nerves even more on edge.

He waded into the water and put her things into his craft. 'Hop in.'

Giselle stood her ground. 'I'm perfectly capable of sailing back by myself.' She tried to sound mature and calm and confident.

His smile gave no quarter. 'But you'll come back with me,' he said, and this time there was no mistaking the threat. 'I don't like peeping Toms—or Thomasinas—and I want to find out why no one warned you to keep off the island.'

Obstinately she insisted, 'I want to sail back.'

'And I want you to come with me,' he said as though that clinched the matter.

When she glared at him he picked her up and dumped her into the small craft, following her in with a lunge that literally rocked the boat.

'Damn you!' she spluttered, totally bewildered by her body's shocking, incandescent response to those few dazzling moments in his arms.

Outrage at his overt use of power against her warred with fierce awareness, primitive and hotly consuming. A charged tension burned through every nerve, the memory of his strength and an elusive, primal scent paralysing any coherent thought.

Her objections were cut off by the roar of the engine. She lurched as the runabout took off, and sat down abruptly where he indicated, ruffled and flaming with a debilitating mixture of embarrassment and anger.

Arrogant, high-handed, overbearing pirate—who the heck was he? The owner of Coconut Bay?

He was certainly formidable, and apparently the prospect of being charged with assault and kidnapping didn't worry him in the least.

Obstinately keeping her head turned away from him, she stared across the vivid waters of the lagoon until the boat slowed as they came into Coconut Bay, her abductor effortlessly threading a way through the swimmers until they reached the beach.

Giselle's suspicions were reinforced by a reception committee—the boatman, the manager of the resort and a couple of other people with carefully neutral expressions.

Her captor was clearly very important.

Confirmation came the moment he cut the engine and swung over the side. The manager stepped forward, smiling. 'Any problems?' he asked, keeping his gaze fixed on the man in the water.

'No,' her tormentor said evenly.

He relinquished care of the craft to the boatman and turned to hold out a commanding hand to Giselle. She stiffened at his unwanted solicitude, and with a proud glare lowered herself into the warm, silken water.

He gave her a mocking glance, then told the manager he'd seen the guest...

'Miss Giselle Foster,' the manager told him, officiously and entirely unnecessarily, Giselle thought indignantly, oddly spooked by the idea of her kidnapper knowing her name.

'Ah. Miss Foster,' he said, with an intonation that sent a little chill chasing another down her spine, a chill his smile did nothing to dispel. He turned back to the manager. 'I was surprised no one had told her that Motukai is private.'

The manager looked at the boatman, silently inviting him to speak. He said quietly, 'I was about to when I heard the mother of the little child call out.'

'Ah,' the manager said swiftly. 'Of course.' He turned to Mr Too-Handsome-For-His-Own-Good, and explained, 'A woman thought her child had disappeared, Your Highness.'

Your Highness!

Who the devil was he? With an effort, Giselle forced her attention back to the manager's respectful explanation.

'It took us several minutes to discover that he'd joined some other children just along the beach and was playing hide and seek with them. We searched the water first, of course. And by then Ms Foster had gone. But I gather she gave the impression that she was going to the next bay. And as we couldn't see the dinghy we didn't realise she'd strayed. I'm very sorry—a genuine mistake all around.'

Giselle stiffened. The way he'd phrased it seemed to indicate she had intentionally sailed off during the search for the child after lying about her destination, then hidden the little craft!

With a warm smile, Giselle addressed the boatman. 'I'm sorry that you were blamed. It won't happen again.' She cast a level, blank glance at the man who'd dragged her back ashore and smiled again, this time making sure it didn't reach her eyes. 'Thank you for making sure I got back safely.' She paused, then said sweetly, 'Oh, and may I have my camera, please?'

'Of course,' he said, just as pleasantly, and removed it from his shirt pocket. His smile taunted her as he handed it over.

Rigid with anger, Giselle put it in her bag, picked up her

hamper and her book, and nodded all around before walking erectly away.

Back in her room she stood motionless for a few seconds, then let out a long ragged breath. That weaselly manager, making it seem as though she'd deliberately lied to them! And of all the arrogant despots, her captor had to take the cake.

His Highness indeed! Somehow she wasn't in the least surprised to find out that he was a prince. She could just see him lording it over the poor islanders, refusing them access, riding roughshod...

In fact, the only one who'd come out of this with any degree of dignity was the boatman.

Still seething, she showered and washed the sand and salt out of her long black hair, wryly amused at herself for trying such a hackneyed way of banishing the whole stupid situation. She hadn't eaten the lunch she'd packed, so she opened the picnic basket and forced down the food without tasting it, her thoughts still in turmoil.

Why had Prince Whoever-He-Was responded so angrily—and outrageously—at the possibility that she might have taken photographs of him and his companion? Were they illicit lovers?

Perhaps they were married, and understandably indignant at the prospect of being photographed while they made love. He'd obviously thought she could be one of the paparazzi. But even that didn't excuse his rudeness.

As if she cared! 'Enough!' she said impatiently into the humid air, and fossicked out her book. 'Forget about it.'

The resort had been cleverly built; it was marketed to a younger crowd without children, those with disposable money, and it was beautiful. The rooms were comfortable and cleverly decorated, each with a small, shaded balcony where two recliners overlooked either gardens bright with hibiscus, the beach, or the pool. Hers faced the beach.

Giselle took her book out and lowered herself into a recliner, determined to lose herself in the riveting story she'd been promised.

Half an hour later she closed the pages. 'Go *away*!' she muttered in an undertone, directing the command to a man who wasn't even there.

She picked up the book and went inside, the midday heat sucking the strength from her body.

Determined to prise that wretched man out of her mind, she swam for half an hour in the lagoon, then slathered herself in sunscreen again, stretched out on one of the loungers beneath a sun umbrella, and tried once more to read.

Several people stopped to chat; she found herself agreeing to go to the Island Night with a couple of women, so as the rapid dusk was overtaken by soft, scented darkness she went with them back to the beach where the staff and some of the local villagers were preparing what she'd been promised was a vigorous, soul-stirring evening's entertainment of song and dance.

Prince Roman Magnati watched Bella Adams slam out of the room. Her marriage as well as her career must be in the doldrums, he thought cynically, wiping off the lipstick that had just missed his mouth. Although, a certain amount of desperation could be excused in a woman whose modelling career depended entirely on her beauty as she approached the dangerous age of thirty.

He hadn't realised that her husband was flying back to America instead of coming on this cruise around Fala'isi. Roman enjoyed the company of beautiful women, but he required intelligence and charm as well. Bella might possess more than her fair share of sophistication, but her idea of an intelligent conversation seemed to be encouraging ever more fulsome compliments about her ethereal beauty.

Roman had principles; he didn't seduce married women—even willing ones—or virgins. And it was a quirk of his to be the pursuer, not the pursued.

It was Bella who'd suggested they visit the islet; he'd assumed that the other guests on board were coming too, only to discover that they'd decided to stay behind. And, from the hint of smugness in her famous smile, he realised she'd had a hand in their decision.

Still irritated, he keyed in a number on the telephone. When his friend Luke Chapman picked it up Roman said without preamble, 'Next time you can do your own dirty work.'

'Having trouble?'

'Nothing I can't handle. How's Fleur?'

He could hear Luke's grin in his tone. 'She's pregnant.'

The next couple of minutes were filled with hearty congratulations, before Luke said, 'I'm sorry about lumbering you with our guests, but Fleur's feeling pretty under the weather at the moment.'

And Luke Chapman was ruthless when it came to protecting his wife. Roman could understand that; he could be ruthless too. 'It was nothing,' he said calmly. 'Bella's packing now, and the other two are charming. I'll deliver them to you tomorrow as arranged.'

'Bella's packing?'

'Yes. I need a chopper to get her to the airport. Is yours in use?'

'You're off Coconut Bay? It'll be there in an hour.'

The Chapmans ruled Fala'isi like benevolent despots; getting rid of an unwelcome guest was no problem.

'Thanks. Give Fleur my love and heartiest congratulations, won't you?'

Accepting Bella as a guest on his yacht had seemed a small thing; Roman had no doubts about his ability to squelch any overt attempts at seduction.

So he'd been coolly pleasant to her, agreeing to apply sunscreen, somewhat cynically amused by her obvious attempts at flirtation. Until he'd caught the movement in the trees and realised they were being watched.

His lip curled. Just as well the dark-haired intruder hadn't taken any photographs. He frowned. Long-limbed and lithe, her skin as white as her hair was black, she'd shown spirit and a rather charming innocence.

Roman walked to a porthole in his cabin, looking out over the lagoon. Tonight he'd planned to take his remaining two guests to the Island Night at the resort; the troupe there was well worth seeing. There'd be dancing—the sensuous hip movements of those dances designed for seduction, followed by dances that told legends, and then fire-dancing with long torches.

His guests had declined the invitation; due to leave the island the next day, they wanted an early night. Nevertheless, Roman decided to go across to the resort after dinner. Giselle Foster would probably be there, and he'd been intrigued and puzzled by a pulse of recognition, a feeling he'd noticed those neat, proud features somewhere before.

If he saw her again, he might get the connection. He didn't like it when his brain let him down.

Besides, even when he'd thought she might be a member of the paparazzi, he'd liked what he'd seen. Very much. Most women, consciously or unconsciously, tried to flirt with him. She hadn't.

'Scratch my eyes out more likely,' he said, irony plain in his tone as he turned back to the computer.

She'd moved with a graceful economy, her body beneath the bikini and sarong hinting at strength and some very intriguing curves, and she had stunning legs.

And that hair! Cruelly yanked back off her face to reveal a face unadorned with anything other than sunscreen, it had flowed like a black waterfall over her shoulders as she'd spun around to confront him.

He thought of that hair on his skin and his body responded with a full, uncompromising alert.

Her features might be no more than neat, but her mouth—ah, her mouth. Full and red, and tilted at the corners, it backed up the secret promise of her eyes, so intense a green they glowed with inner fire.

An indication of hidden passion? Perhaps. It might be interesting to find out. He sat down at his computer and sent off an email to his head of security.

CHAPTER TWO

'HEY,' said one of Giselle's two companions, a sleek redhead called Terry. 'Who's the babe magnet? The tall guy with the broad, broad shoulders and the...*presence*?' She lowered her voice to a husky growl on the last word.

Giselle followed her glance, and felt her stomach drop into emptiness as light from the flaming torches sheened the dark head of her nemesis. Blood tingling through her veins, she wished she'd given in to that instinct to stay snug in her room and finish her book. Her throat dried, and she needed a cold shower.

Or to run.

Instead, she swallowed. 'I believe he's a prince.' And, because keeping silent might seem odd, she added casually, 'He brought me back from one of the little islands when I accidentally trespassed there today.'

'And you didn't find out his *name*?' The other woman with her, an uninhibited blonde with the improbable name of Bibi, sent her an incredulous look. 'Why? Did all that male gorgeousness strike you dumb?'

Mentally shrugging, Giselle gave a swift, emotionless run-down without mentioning the man's companion.

Who didn't seem to be with him tonight.

Terry gave a huge sigh. 'Wow, a trespasser and a pirate. Just like a chick movie.'

Giselle's smile was ironic. 'Not one I want to star in; he wasn't exactly welcoming,' she said dryly.

'It must have been so romantic.' Bibi's eyes were fixed avidly on the prince's arrogant, aquiline features.

No, Giselle thought with a little shiver, it hadn't been romantic. He wasn't a man to flirt with; for a few seconds she'd been intimidated by the cold threat she sensed beneath that handsome exterior. And even now, clad in perfectly tailored, casual clothes made to fit those broad shoulders and long legs, smiling as he talked to several of the performers, he exuded an aura of forbidding, controlled power that backed up his inherent sensuality. In this assembly of lithe, tanned men, he stood out.

Terry breathed, 'He is *breathtaking*!' Her brow wrinkled. 'Hang on, I've seen him in some magazine or other.'

She rummaged through her brain while Giselle sipped her drink, trying to look no more than mildly interested.

'I remember!' her chatty companion said, alight with triumph. 'He's one of the Considines. Actually, he's not, but he is definitely a prince. Something to do with the sea.'

'A Pacific prince?' Giselle asked wryly. The name Considine rang a faint bell in her mind.

Terry gave a gurgle of laughter. 'No, no, a European one—well, a Mediterranean one. He's related to the Considines—the Illyrian royal family. There was an article in one of the magazines about him; now that really *was* romantic. One of his ancestors—a Considine princess—was sort of kidnapped by the ruler of some islands off the coast of Illyria and held as a hostage in his castle.'

Just in time Giselle stopped herself from remarking that

kidnapping seemed to run in the family. 'It sounds pretty frightening, actually.'

'Well, she was beautiful—'

'All princesses are, by definition,' Giselle returned smartly.

Terry grinned. 'Don't be so cynical. And if he was anything like this prince I'll bet she couldn't believe her luck! He can kidnap me any time he likes. Anyway, handsome or not, they fell in love and were married.'

To Giselle, the story seemed like a gloss manufactured by later generations of a family to soften a situation that had probably been brutally political and not at all comfortable for the woman at the centre of it.

On a long, envious sigh, Bibi, who held an important job in some esoteric financial think-tank, chimed in, 'Of course—he's Prince Roman Magnati! He's royalty in the business world, too. Utterly brilliant, and truly loaded.' She pressed a hand to her heart. 'But none of that means a thing compared to his glamour, does it? On the delectability scale he must be a twenty out of ten! And you *know* him!'

Appalled by the possibility that both women were going to ask her to introduce them to the prince, Giselle blurted, 'I really don't know him!'

Anyway, *delectable* wasn't a word she'd use to describe him. It failed to convey the unconscious assurance he wielded like a sword. Frowning, she tried to work out what made the prince—if he really was a prince—so…so dominant.

Good genes helped, of course, but it wasn't just the fact that he was handsome. As basic as the magnificent framework of his face was his air of compelling, almost imperious power, formidable and uncompromising. Few princes of the blood had that, and even fewer the forceful physicality that burned beneath his coolly sophisticated exterior.

A stray thought popped into Giselle's brain, startling her

into a swift flush. Part of his attraction—to women, anyway—had to be an instinctive, purely feminine recognition that he'd be a brilliant lover.

On the other hand, instinct had been known to let people down; he might be as surly and ill-tempered in bed as he'd been to her on the beach, she thought sturdily, dragging her eyes away from his dark head and fixing them on the dancers.

'So he's Illyrian?' she remarked, hoping her casual tone sounded unforced.

'Sure is,' Bibi told her. 'Lord of the Sea Isles. Well, that's what his father was before that dictator took over Illyria. I think his mother was a Russian grand duchess, descended from their royal family. She was a concert pianist—a very good one—but she died young. So did his father.'

Drums throbbed into action, calling their attention back to the second part of the show. The Polynesian people of the Pacific had a great and warlike past they were proud of, and the villagers showed the guests a pot-pourri of the skills that had made them such feared warriors.

One particular mock combat, with long spears made of some black wood, heavily carved and decorated with a tuft of black and white feathers, was especially fierce. Fascinated, Giselle watched as the men's glistening bodies whirled and leapt in the light of the torches, thrusting and parrying in half-dance, half-aggression until one man gained an advantage and the other yielded.

To wild applause the two men pulled back. They called for volunteers, and when a couple of the more outgoing men in the audience came up, showed them the actions before conducting a mock bout.

A movement caught the corner of Giselle's eye; she turned slightly to see an elderly, white-haired islander approach Prince Roman. The older man said something to him, nodding at the stage. The prince smiled, but gave a small shake of his head.

The elderly islander didn't try to persuade him, or shame him into it. Grinning, he said something that brought a swift, laughing reply from the taller man.

A tiny incident, yet it said something about the prince, Giselle thought reluctantly, returning her attention to the stage where the volunteers postured and parried. In spite of the aura of mastery and decisiveness that warned onlookers he was not to be messed with, Roman Magnati had the common touch.

Afterwards the performers coaxed more people up onto the low stage and persuaded them to dance. It was all good-humoured, and people joined in with enthusiasm, although Giselle was startled when one of the women from the troupe came over and beckoned her up.

'Go on, be a sport,' her two companions encouraged in chorus.

Normally she wouldn't have worried about making a fool of herself, but tonight it was the last thing she wanted to do. She didn't have to look across the crowd, laughing and rowdily enjoying the show, to know why.

Irritated with herself, she said, 'All right,' and got to her feet, along with, she was glad to see, several other women.

She thought that they'd go up as they were, but they were hustled into a makeshift dressing room where brightly coloured cloths were wound around their breasts and hips, garlands of flowers and leaves slung around their necks, and then with much laughter they were swept out onto the stage.

Acutely self-conscious, and aware of the wide expanse of bare skin around her midriff, Giselle concentrated on the dance.

It was simple enough, although she'd never in a thousand years be able to achieve the beautiful hand gestures, or the sexy hip movements. However, by concentrating on their leader, she managed not to think of Prince Roman Magnati watching her. Relief flooded her when at last the drums stopped, and everyone laughed and cheered them and clapped.

'Good dancer,' one of the local women said, nodding when it was over. 'You got the style, girl. You should have been born here, and you'd have learned how to do the hula before you could walk.'

Giselle laughed, pink with exertion and pleasure at the compliment. In spite of the prince's presence, a burr of awareness beneath her skin, the evening had been fun—the entertainment skilful and slick, and the singing that followed sweet enough to carry her to heaven.

'You can't go now,' Terry protested later, when Giselle picked up her bag. 'There'll be dancing any minute—look, the band's just arrived.'

Giselle had learned to dance at high school, but the last time she'd taken the floor was at the school ball in her final year of school.

'I think I'll give it a miss,' she said lightly as the band began to tune their instruments. 'Trespassing is tiring work.'

In spite of their protests, she threaded her way between the dancers. She was a few metres away from the dance floor, stepping onto the sand beneath the palms where tables and chairs waited for those who decided to sit out, when a tell-tale prickle of sensation ran from the top of her head to the base of her spine. Her breath stopped; dimly she was aware that the band had just swung into a vigorous, bouncy song perfect for luring people onto the floor.

From too close behind, Giselle heard a voice—deep and almost sardonic. 'Ah, Giselle Foster. Going so soon?'

Giselle froze, heart hammering in an oddly disconnected rhythm in her chest. She felt extremely wary, yet stimulated, as though the prince had churned up unknown emotions.

And hormones. Her breath came faster through her lips and her eyes widened as she turned her head to look at him, resenting his power to summon such a primal physical response from her reluctant body.

'Yes,' she said, making no attempt to qualify her blunt answer.

Roman Magnati's smile sent little shivers of excitement skidding from nerve to nerve. He knew the effect he was having on her; he probably expected women to swoon at his feet.

'So it's no use asking you to dance,' he said smoothly.

Giselle blinked. As her godmother said occasionally, *Morals are important, but manners are vital.*

Reluctantly she returned his smile, careful not to let it reach her eyes. 'Unfortunately I'd have had to refuse,' she said, her tone far too sweet. 'We haven't been introduced.'

His eyes narrowed for a fraction of a second, then to her chagrin she saw laughter glint in their midnight darkness. 'Oh, we can find someone to do that,' he said, and held out his hand, taking away any options she might have had. 'Or, failing that, I can tell you that I am Roman Magnati, an Illyrian. I know that you are a New Zealander, and that your mother was a romantic.'

Her lashes flew up. 'What…?'

'Giselle is such a romantic name,' he explained, hand still outstretched.

After a moment's hesitation Giselle took it. His grip was warm and firm, and he didn't crush her fingers or hold it for too long. Nevertheless, shaking hands with Prince Roman Magnati was like being subjected to an electric shock, one that ricocheted through her with the devastating impact of lightning.

She flinched. So her response when he'd dumped her in his boat hadn't been an aberration; somehow this man set every cell in her body alive and clamouring.

He let her hand go immediately. 'I'm sorry,' he said, his voice subtly amused. 'Did I hurt you?'

Of course he knew he hadn't. Without looking at him she said, 'No.' Her voice sounded weird—high and strained—so she started again. 'No, I'm fine.'

'It's probably the heat,' he told her. 'A lot of people don't realise how debilitating the Tropics can be.' He looked over her head and said, 'A glass of lime juice, please.'

'I'm fine,' she repeated, steadying her tone and feeling rather desperate. 'And I'm not in the least thirsty.'

But he took her elbow and somehow she found herself walking with him towards a table and chairs set on the edge of the sand. 'That's one of the symptoms of dehydration— a lack of thirst. Can you remember when you last had a drink—and I don't mean tea or coffee, or anything with alcohol in it.'

Did he think she was drunk? 'I've had one glass of wine with dinner and a rather nasty fruit cocktail,' she said stonily.

'And you've been dancing.'

He sat her down. Scrabbling for an excuse—any excuse, however stupid—to get out of there, she said, 'Look, you're being very kind but I'm tired. I'll have something to drink in my room.'

'Once you've reassured me that I don't have to worry about dehydration I'll escort you there.'

He spoke quite gently, but his tone indicated that he meant it. With prickly resignation, she decided that making a fuss wasn't at all sophisticated. She'd drink the damned lime juice, then go to her room.

She could, of course, walk away. So why didn't she? Because he wasn't being rude. And possibly, she realised incredulously, because being cared for was so unexpected.

Her father had been an undemonstrative man who'd expected her to look after herself. This man's concern for her welfare homed in on an undiscovered weakness.

Anyway, she might as well do what her godmother would want—enjoy for a few minutes the company of the best-looking man she'd ever seen. Besides, if she went on refusing he'd know for sure that her odd reaction to his touch wasn't dehydration…

Uneasily aware of his scrutiny, she realised she was storing impressions, taking in the sweet, seductive perfume of the frangipani bush close by, and the soft salt tang of the sea.

And the way the light fell across Prince Roman's barbaric cheekbones, picking out the hard, intensely masculine framework of his face.

Irritated, she said coolly, 'Has anyone ever mentioned that perhaps you might be a trifle overbearing?'

She caught his white smile in the mellow darkness as he sat down opposite her. 'It has been suggested occasionally,' he admitted blandly.

The waiter appeared with two glasses, setting one down before her and the other in front of the prince. And he didn't ask for ID, so either Roman Magnati was a regular visitor, or he had some position at the resort. The owner perhaps?

Giselle said, 'You didn't bring your companion with you tonight?'

'She is not my companion.' He leaned back in the chair to examine her. 'She was a guest on my yacht, along with several others.'

His voice was level, perfectly steady, yet Giselle discerned a thread of steel running through the words.

Oh, yeah? she thought inelegantly.

So what was with smoothing the sunscreen so seductively onto her back, then? The unknown, vaguely familiar woman certainly didn't think herself as a mere guest, not if her arch looks and purring little stretches had been anything to go by.

And his tone carried an unspoken warning.

She picked up her glass and sipped, her suddenly dry throat welcoming the cool liquid. It emboldened her to say, 'Are you on a Pacific cruise?'

'For a few days.'

'I notice everyone knows you here, so I presume you're a regular visitor?'

Even in the darkness she saw one brow lift. 'I am friendly with the resort's owners, and have been here a couple of times before,' he drawled, his tone courteous yet making her feel she'd pried. 'Where do you live in New Zealand?'

Reluctantly she told him, 'In the north.'

'Ah, a very beautiful part of the country. In Whangarei?'

His knowledge of the biggest town in Northland—a very small city—surprised her. 'About an hour further north,' she said reluctantly.

'On a farm?'

Well, no doubt she looked a hick. She sipped more lime juice before saying distantly, 'Yes.'

He surprised her again by asking, 'You enjoy the life?'

Shrugging, she evaded the question. 'It keeps me busy.'

'I imagine it must,' he said, almost as if his mind was on something else.

It probably was. Well, it served him right if he was bored; he'd forced the issue here. But it didn't seem fair when she was so recklessly aware of the physical fallout from his touch, his nearness, and the compelling impact of his presence.

He lifted his glass to his mouth, drank, and set it down again. 'What made you decide to make farming your career?'

Career? 'Circumstances mainly,' she said frankly. 'And I love P—my home; it's utterly beautiful.'

'Have you lived there all your life?'

She nodded and sipped more of her drink. Literally; she'd even been born at Parirua. The oldest of twins, she'd arrived a little earlier than planned. Her sister Leola had been less impetuous, timing her arrival for after they'd been safely helicoptered to hospital.

At the thought of her sister Giselle's brows pleated. For the last month she'd sensed that something was wrong with Leola; she was miserable. Not that she admitted to anything, getting quite snappy the night before Giselle left for Fala'isi when she'd tried to persuade Leola to tell her what the problem was.

'And do you have siblings?' the prince asked, his tone idle.

Her mother hadn't wanted any more children. Life on a cattle station had been far too uncivilised for her. Giselle forestalled any further questions by asking, 'Do you?'

'A brother,' he said smoothly. 'Several years younger.'

'That probably explains it.'

He laughed, revealing very white teeth and an almost indecent charm. 'My tendency to be overbearing? Perhaps. But I'm asking too many questions. So what would you like to know about me?'

Having the tables turned on her rendered her temporarily speechless. She stared at him, caught a glint of something that could have been mockery in his eyes, and was glad that it was dark and he couldn't see the heat in her skin.

'I told you where I was born,' she said, 'so it's only fair that you should tell me where you were.'

'In a clinic in Switzerland. My parents were exiles; my mother from Russia, and my father from Illyria.'

'Did he go back to Illyria once the dictator died?'

'No. He was murdered by Paulo Considine's agents before that.'

'Murdered?' She gazed at him in shock, and saw the mask of masculine beauty transformed into something grimmer, a warrior's face, cold and ruthless and filled with concentrated power.

'Poisoned,' he said succinctly. 'Because he was working actively to make the dictator an outcast. He was killed before he knew how well he'd succeeded.'

Shaken, she sipped more of her drink and unexpectedly found herself thinking of Parirua and the life she lived there. It seemed very safe.

'That was atrocious and utterly cowardly,' she said thinly. 'I'm very sorry.'

'So am I. Very sorry that I wasn't able to get to Paulo Considine and make him suffer even a fraction of what my father suffered.'

His voice was measured, but Giselle found herself shivering at its lethal flatness.

She was relieved when he went on, 'However, I'm fortunate to be in a position to help undo some of the harm he did.' He smiled, and that compelling charm cloaked the warrior once more.

Until then, Giselle realised, she hadn't really accepted that he was a prince. Although the whole concept of royalty seemed too outrageous, the man on the other side of the table really did have the right to call himself Prince.

But what had totally unnerved her was that flash of

cold, uncompromising and completely intimidating authority. This man was dangerous, and so far out of her world that he might as well be from Mars.

'How are you doing that?' she asked tentatively, watching his broad shoulders lift and settle.

'My cousin Alex asked me to move back to Illyria to the islands that were our ancient fiefdom. They were the scenes of the dictator's most repressive regime. Even though he knew that the soil on most of the islands is too poor to grow anything but olive trees and vines, he forbade any fishing and had every boat sunk so that the people couldn't escape across the sea to Italy. This caused hideous famines, much death and misery. With representatives of the people I am setting up a fishing industry and a plan for tourism.'

'Is that why you're here?' she asked. 'Researching?'

Ah, she'd managed to surprise him this time, and that, she thought snidely, didn't say much for his taste in women.

'Partly,' he conceded. 'Fala'isi could so easily have lapsed into another small, poor Pacific nation, but thanks to the Chapman family's foresight and good business brains it is flourishing, and without wrecking the ancient social structure. I want to make sure something like this happens on my lands before I die.'

This was a dynastic thing. Giselle's grandfather would have understood; perhaps even her father, who'd wanted sons to follow him at Parirua. She'd always known she was very second best.

No doubt the prince wanted heirs too, but then he probably had women lining up for the honour of having his children, whereas her father had never recovered from her mother's desertion. If he couldn't have the woman he loved, he wanted no other.

'You don't agree?' the prince drawled.

Giselle realised that she'd let the silence drag on too long. 'On the contrary, I think it's a very worthy aim.'

He smiled again, and she saw the practised charmer, the man who accepted his effect on women without conceit. Not, she thought, that any lack of conceit would stop him from using that potent male charisma if he thought it expedient.

As, for some unknown reason, he had been doing for the past few minutes. Giselle had no illusions about herself. Oh, she was tall, and she had a good figure, and her features were neat, but on the dance floor behind them were at least twenty other women who were not only better looking, but had infinitely more sexual allure. In this tropical ambience of dark-haired women her long black hair didn't stand out, but, because softly golden skins were the norm here, her pallor certainly did, unfortunately in a most un-chic way.

Yet he was taking time and effort to charm her.

Again she wondered about the identity of the woman she'd seen him with on the beach.

So when he said, 'And are you happy on your farm? Is that your life's ambition?' she looked up, startled, and met those darkly blue eyes, oddly intent and penetrating.

Her skin tightened, and every tiny hair lifted in the age-old indication of danger.

'Who knows what the future might bring?' she said, then tried to cover her curtness by draining her glass and setting it back on the table.

'So dance the night away?' he asked, his words faintly contemptuous.

With a glittering smile, she got to her feet, only to find him rising with her. He was so much taller that he made her feel weak and fragile, an experience that was new to her. 'Oh, do so by all means, but I'll pass, thanks.'

'Then you must allow me to escort you to your room,' he said, his tone brooking no refusal.

'That's not necessary.'

'Nevertheless, I will do so.'

Baulked, she drew in a long, steadying breath. His voice—cool, determined, amused—told her she wasn't going to get her own way; it would be quicker and simpler to give in.

'Right, if you must, then let's go,' she said serenely, hoping her voice betrayed neither her irritation at his high-handedness nor the forbidden, reckless agitation that was setting her nerves on fire.

The resort seemed almost deserted as they walked along paths of coral sand, the music muted once they'd put a couple of buildings between them and the dance floor. It was a perfect evening, the soft thunder of the long Pacific combers on the reef echoing in her ears. The moon hadn't risen yet, and in the crushed velvet sky the stars shone like diamonds, so big she thought she could reach out and pick them if she had the courage.

She was singularly lacking there, she thought flatly. Maura would despair of her. If she was brave she'd be dancing with Prince Roman Magnati instead of walking towards her solitary bed. She'd be flirting—if she knew how. She might even be expecting a kiss…

Whoa! That wouldn't be courageous—that would be dangerous stupidity. And so was the way her mind lingered on the thought, spinning sexy fantasies, drinking in the night and the sensuous signals it was sending.

Fortunately, before she could get hung up on the way the prince walked—like a panther, silently graceful and predatory—or the way his fingers on her skin were sending torrid little quivers of anticipation through her, she managed to quench her inner turmoil by thinking of the other women he could have asked to dance.

Why had he chosen her? There had to be a reason, because not only was she not a patch on them in looks, but she didn't have much in the way of social graces, either. In contrast to the sleekly fashionable resort clothes the other women wore, she'd chosen a cheap pareu from the hotel shop in dark green with highlights of silver that echoed her sandals.

Yet he'd targeted her, which might well have something to do with the scene she'd witnessed on the beach. No, that didn't make sense.

And he hadn't apologised for his autocratic behaviour—hadn't even mentioned it.

So what the heck did you say to a man who had the world at his feet when you said goodbye after sharing a drink?

She set her jaw. Not a lot—just make it pleasant, distant and quick.

At the base of the stairs leading to her floor, she stopped and said, 'This is my block. Thank you.'

'I'll come with you to your door,' he said, and smiled down at her.

Roman could see he'd irritated her, but he suspected she didn't know why he wanted to know what room she was in. He was almost convinced she was who she'd said she was; his security team had run a quick check on her and she'd come up clean, and exactly the person she'd claimed to be. So why was she so cagy?

He watched the tiny frown between her winged black brows smooth out and her face go blank.

'There's no need,' she said, her voice level.

'I'll feel better. I was harsh to you this afternoon; I'd like to apologise.'

She seemed to accept that. 'You presumably had your reasons,' she said dispassionately, and went up the stairs with him.

Outside her room he waited while she unlocked the door. He said abruptly, 'You're too trusting. You don't know me.'

'Short of yelling for Security, I couldn't get rid of you,' she pointed out, adding with a sly note of mockery, 'Anyway, one of the women I was with vouched for you. She reads women's magazines and I don't. I'm sure I'm quite safe.'

He said austerely, 'There have been more than a few princes whose morals don't bear scrutiny.'

'But you wouldn't have sat in public with me for half an hour if you'd been plotting my ruin. The waiter saw us together.'

Roman prided himself on his complete control over his temper, but for some reason her ironic, dismissive words ruffled him. He said sardonically, 'And waiters the world over have been known to accept money for conveniently seeing nothing.'

She pushed the door open and turned to face him. 'Goodnight,' she said stiffly.

From the first moment he'd seen her face Roman had been intrigued by her; even when he'd thought she might be some sort of paparazzo he'd wanted to kiss that firm, lush mouth, feel it soften against his in surrender. Beside her, Bella Adams' polished sexuality had been shown up for the fake it was, a cloak donned whenever she wanted to dazzle.

This woman in her simple sarong and cheap sandals had no artifice, yet when she walked it was with a natural grace that somehow bypassed his excellent defences.

And that irritated him; Roman knew that the world was full of beautiful women, many of whom wanted something from him. This one was prickly and ungracious, with a sense of humour so dry it was close to arid. Not his style at all.

Perhaps he'd become jaded and degenerate, got to the stage where he wanted only those women who didn't want him. He enjoyed a challenge, but not with women; he didn't want to break hearts. His lovers had always been so-phisticated women who knew the rules and kept to them.

But when Giselle started to close the door, he put out a hand and pushed it back.

Her eyes darkened. She said tightly, 'I hope this isn't going to turn into an undignified struggle.'

'I hope so too,' he said, and pulled her into his arms and kissed her.

CHAPTER THREE

GISELLE tried to wrench herself free, but he kissed her like a conqueror, barely shielding the raw force of power. Yielding to that masterful sensory assault, her body refused to accept orders. It was too busy responding to the sinful expertise of Roman's kiss.

And after a few seconds her mind stopped sending out commands; it yielded and she shuddered, her bones melting, her body afire with delight and a fierce, basic hunger she couldn't control.

He tasted so good, she thought dazedly, her hands lifting to cling to his shoulders. And he smelt clean, with a faint musky undernote that homed onto some primitively responsive part of her. Desire sang through her with piercing intensity, clamorous and potent, stripping her of every inhibition in the need to lose herself in his touch, his nearness.

He said something in a harsh, shaken voice, words she didn't understand, then settled her into his arms, one arm pinning her hips against him so that she felt the full impact of his need. His mouth on hers obliterated all thought, everything but this wild longing.

She had never felt so alive, and she gave an indistinct murmur, half appeal, half protest.

He took the opportunity to deepen the kiss. Locked against him, she was recklessly aware of the powerful strength of his body, poised and predatory, of how big he was, and how solidly muscled. Breasts crushed against him, stomach knotting in a kind of divine tension, she reacted at a subliminal level to every subtle coil and flex of his body.

A glimmer of panic fought mindless instinct, then was submerged in a primitive, more dangerous reaction.

He raised his head, but only to kiss the corner of her mouth, then find the lobe of one ear and bite delicately. A pang of helpless, deliciously elemental response shot through her so that she sagged against him, her surrender complete.

And then she was set back, and he said on a raw note, 'People are coming. Either we go inside, or I leave.'

Dimly, eyes huge and shadowed in a white face as she scanned the dark planes and arrogant angles of his, she realised she could hear voices. At the foot of the stairs. Laughter...

Humiliation shattering the last pathetic remnants of her composure, she said in a stunned, embarrassed voice, 'You—leave.'

He looked at her for a tense second, his big body poised and feral; she saw him reimpose control, incline his head in a mocking bow, and step back so that she could close the door.

Shamed to the core, she slammed the door. She'd been so overwhelmed by his kisses that a palm tree could have fallen on her and she wouldn't have noticed.

But he hadn't lost his head or his sense of proportion or his common sense. He'd heard the voices and been able to pull back, because he hadn't any emotion invested in those savagely tender kisses.

She leaned back against the door, panting as though she'd spent a day drafting cattle.

Dear God, she'd been easy, so *easy*, melting into his arms like jelly. He was probably laughing on his way back to that gorgeous yacht—or perhaps he was heading for the dance floor again to pick up someone else, someone just as willing but who had more experience.

At least she could say she'd been kissed by a prince, she thought sardonically, stiffening her shoulders and her legs so that she could move away from the door. Not many women could boast of that—although maybe she was wrong there. Judging by his proficiency, Prince Roman Magnati had honed his natural talent on hundreds.

But why had he kissed her?

Later, sleepless in the warm tropical night, she found herself going over and over the question. She must have irritated him with her eagerness to get away, but why hadn't he shrugged those broad shoulders and gone on his way?

Instead he'd used the power of his sexuality as punishment.

And it had been cruel of him, she thought, awash with renewed shame, to prolong it when she'd responded. Surely he'd realised she was totally out of her depth?

Why should he care? No doubt he was used to an entirely different reaction from women.

He probably thought that would teach her to spy on him and his girlfriend. And it wasn't as though they'd ever meet again, or that he'd remember her even if they did.

It should have been a comforting thought; instead, to her horror, tears prickled the back of her eyes, and she had to swallow hard.

Her godmother, she thought grittily, would probably consider the experience a necessary part of growing up. Perhaps she'd be right; Giselle had waited long enough to feel the feverish surge of passion.

It had come with a price, though. Desire had its own

secrets, its own power, and she'd just discovered herself to be defenceless against it.

Watching the stars wheel high in a sky as dark and fathomless as Roman's eyes, she thought of the few boys she'd kissed, their fumbling caresses persuading her that she simply wasn't a sexual being.

Ha! One kiss from a dark-haired, dark-eyed prince with a killer smile had smashed that theory into smithereens! Was this how her mother had felt when she'd left her husband and children for a man she'd known only a few weeks? As though life without him was shatteringly incomplete…as though he'd somehow opened up a vista of horizons and pleasure she'd never known to exist?

'If that's so, I don't want anything to do with it,' she said quietly into her silent room.

Because in the end it meant nothing. Three years after so carelessly snatching her mother's heart away, her lover had dumped her. Alone and betrayed, every cent she'd got from her share of Parirua gone, she'd taken an overdose of painkillers and died alone in a cheap hotel bedroom on the other side of the world.

Giselle woke the next morning with a headache and the firm decision that she'd have nothing more to do with Roman Magnati. If he turned up at the resort again she'd run like hell in the opposite direction—she just wasn't equipped to deal with such a high-powered marauder.

Not that he would, of course. Last night must have been some sort of aberration for him; according to Bibi and Terry, he was noted for his exquisitely beautiful girlfriends. And if the one on the beach was any indication, they were right.

Giselle had no illusions about her looks. Leola, her sophisticated sister, told her that she didn't make the most of herself, but, as Giselle always pointed out, she didn't have her sister's instinctive sense of style.

'Because you've never cared enough to try,' Leola told her crisply.

Which was true, but her life didn't lead to an interest in fashion or beauty.

And she wasn't going to start developing one now. That would make Prince Roman Magnati and his sizzling kisses too important. Instead, she'd continue with the routine she'd established. A swim in the lagoon first, then breakfast...

But on the way back from her swim she met Bibi on the beach, and had to suffer her scrutiny, bright with curiosity. 'Hi, you secretive thing, you! Did you know there's a magazine in the shop that has a spread on the prince? What did you think of him?'

'He's certainly dishy,' Giselle said as lightly as she could. 'And he seemed quite nice.'

She refused to discuss him further, but the morning revealed that just about everyone at the resort had either heard some account of the prince bringing her back from the island, or had seen them sitting at that wretched table together on the beach.

Later that day, shamefaced but determined, she waited in the shop until it was empty of customers and bought the magazine, hiding it in her bag while she strode back to her room.

He photographed well, she thought when she'd read the article, trying to be dispassionate. Although the interview was informative about his hopes and plans for his huge estates in Illyria, he'd obviously embargoed any discussion of his personal life. His wealth and influence and power were skimmed over, almost taken for granted.

However, there were photographs of him with various

stunning women wearing superb clothes and jewels. One she looked at with a jolt; frowning, she peered more closely.

The woman beside him could have been Leola. Back to the camera, she was tall and slender and blonde, but a second glance revealed the truth. Leola might perhaps have found herself at a party attended by the prince, but her personal style was edgy and dramatic, and this woman wore what seemed to be a pretty, very conventional dress with sparkles.

Definitely not Leola, then. She wouldn't be seen dead in anything so traditional, Giselle thought with a grin. And it wasn't really likely that an unknown dress designer—almost an apprentice—should go to a party like the one pictured.

Altogether the article was an innocuous effort—respectful, spiced with wit, and with an undertone of deep appreciation of all that Prince Roman Magnati had to offer a woman.

Cross with herself for succumbing to the temptation to buy it, she threw the magazine into the bin and went out to lose herself in her book. When that didn't work she forced herself to join in some of the activities she'd ignored until then. But whatever she did she couldn't drive the prince—or the memory of his kisses—out of her mind.

And some time in the next couple of days she was both infuriated and frustrated to realise that she was acutely strung-up, waiting for him to reappear.

'You can't be addicted!' she told herself angrily.

Of course not! To rid herself of that unnerving sense of emptiness, she flung herself into more of the activities the resort offered, snorkelling and diving in the lagoon and around the reef, dancing at night until she was exhausted, even playing tennis though she hadn't picked up a racquet for years.

At least all the activity meant she slept at night, and if

her dreams were disturbed by the image of a tall, arrogantly handsome prince, they slid away each morning leaving behind nothing but embarrassment.

Until five days before she was due to go back home. After a wrestling match outside her door the previous night with a man who seemed to believe that two dances, the price of a drink, and some rather boring conversation entitled him to a lease on her body and bed for the night, she decided to give up the frenetic socialising and spend the rest of her time on her own.

So she was in her room when the phone rang. Frowning at the kick of anticipation in her heartbeat, she lifted the receiver. Her stomach lurched when she heard the voice of the man she'd left in charge at Parirua.

'What's wrong, Joe?' she asked swiftly.

He coughed. 'You said if anything came in the mail that looked important to let you know.'

'Yes. What is it?'

'It's a letter from the tax people. The Inland Revenue. It's addressed to your father.'

She frowned. 'Dad?' Although her father had left the station's finances in a huge mess, she was certain she'd managed to get everything in order for the tax department. It was probably one of their newsletters. 'You'd better open it and read it to me.'

'OK.'

While he was opening it he told her that everything on the station was under control and the weather was good. 'Too dry, but the water's holding up well though we'll need rain soon.' Then he started to read out the letter.

He stopped after the first sentence. 'Giselle, this doesn't look good.'

'Keep going,' she said unevenly.

When he'd finished she swallowed. The sick feeling in her stomach had intensified into stunned panic. 'Joe, I'm going to have to sell the station. I can't—I can't raise that sort of money, certainly not in the three weeks they've allowed for payment!'

'I know,' he said in a blank voice that showed his shock. 'It's just about more than the station's worth. Especially right now, with the property market hitting rock-bottom. What happened? What's this trust thing?'

She swallowed. 'I don't know—I didn't know anything about it, and there wasn't anything in his papers. I think he must have set up a trust overseas and been channelling money into it without the IRD's knowledge. Now they want back taxes and penalty taxes.' She drew in a ragged breath. 'I think—you and Rangi had better start looking for other jobs.'

'Rangi can do what he wants,' he said stoutly, 'but you're not going to be able to manage Parirua by yourself, so I'll be staying until it's sold.' He hesitated, then said anxiously, 'How could your father have got things into such a mess?'

'According to that letter, he cheated,' she said stonily.

'He was as honest as the day is long!'

'I know, I know.' She gave a gasping sob, then fought for control. In a steadier voice she said, 'He probably just didn't do things properly. After Grandad died Dad decided he didn't need an accountant.' She was struck by something else and said almost pleadingly, 'Joe, the letter reads as though he knew about the tax audit. Do you think...is it possible he drove off the road deliberately?'

Joe hesitated. 'I don't know,' he said uncertainly. 'I hate to think he'd choose to leave you and Parirua in such a mess, but—I just don't know, Ellie.'

'I'll come home as soon as I can get a flight,' she said, making up her mind.

'You will not! You've been sick, girl! They've given you three weeks to pay; you stay there for the rest of your holiday. It's only four days.'

'Yes,' she said dully. And changing her flight would cost money.

'Well, you can do what you need to do by phone from there. Weren't you made an offer by some big overseas firm a month or so ago? Mega-something?'

'MegaCorp,' she supplied automatically. Smugly sure she'd be able to keep Parirua going, she'd turned the offer down. 'Only it isn't really called that—it's just a sarcastic name I made up for them. You know how I feel about overseas companies coming in and buying up our land. They have another much more distinguished name.'

'Yeah, well, I do remember the land agent's name— same as mine. Joseph Smith, from that big firm in Auckland. Get him on the phone and tell him you're ready to talk business.'

To her horror her throat closed and she couldn't continue.

'Giselle? You there?' Joe sounded worried.

'Yes,' she managed to say. 'Yes, I'll do that. I'm sorry, Joe.'

'It isn't *your* fault,' he said briskly. 'If you come home early, girl, I'll run you off the place. You stay there and soak up the sun and let that agent do all the work. You're not going to be any use to anyone if you get pneumonia again.'

'All right. Thank you for letting me know.'

Giselle put the receiver back onto the cradle and dragged in a deep, jagged breath. Three weeks to find a fortune.

She felt as though she'd been hit with a sandbag. This was the end of the life she loved, but she couldn't give in to emotion because she had responsibilities. Joe and Rangi both had young families, and lived in the station cottages; losing their jobs would be a disaster for them.

She sat down and made a list of people she'd have to telephone, starting with the estate agent who'd contacted her about selling Parirua, and the person from the Inland Revenue who'd signed the letter.

Two hours later, she forced herself to drink a glass of water, then walked out onto her balcony and looked sightlessly across the lagoon. The tax person had been courteous, even sympathetic, telling her that she could appeal but it wasn't likely she'd win. The enormous amount of back tax would have to be paid. Already her father's estate was incurring crippling penalties that he had no authority to waive.

The estate agent had been eager to contact MegaCorp—whatever its name was—and do a deal. She just hoped the organisation was still interested in buying the station, and as soon as possible.

Whatever happened, Parirua was no longer her home, her life or her career.

And she still had to tell Leola, who was back in London after a trip to Paris to take in the collections there. Not now; it was too late to wake her. Besides, there was nothing her sister could do.

And, although she'd be shocked and sympathetic, she wouldn't be as shattered as Giselle. Her life was in the esoteric world of fashion, about as far from the earthy realities of life in Parirua as anything was; one day she'd be a world-famous designer.

At the moment she was working for one in London, gaining the skills and experience to start her own firm in New Zealand.

Later that afternoon, Giselle sprawled out beside the pool, book face-down on her stomach, her eyelids drooping so that the sun on the surface of the water was refracted into golden diamonds through her lashes. A haze of disconnected, turbulent thoughts drifted across her mind until something—a kind of alteration to the atmosphere, a subtle shift of atoms and electrons—pulled every fine, unseen hair on her skin upright.

At first she froze, then as slowly as she dared lifted her lashes against the sun's evening dazzle. She didn't have to open them far to see the man standing on the opposite side of the pool. Tall and dark and disturbing, he was watching her with an intensity that stopped the breath in her throat.

A rush of adrenalin filled her; it took all of her control to lie there pretending she hadn't seen him. She knew Prince Roman Magnati was hunting, and she was in his sights.

Instead of being terrified she was filled by a stark, fierce pleasure that astonished her as much as it gave her courage. In four days she'd be going back to a life she hadn't chosen and an insecure future.

And she'd never before met a man she wanted as much as she wanted Roman Magnati. Damn it, she was still a virgin!

Other women had one-night stands—swift, spur-of-the-minute relationships, if they could be called that. Why shouldn't she?

If—*if*—that was what Roman Magnati wanted, she'd agree. For once in her life, she thought boldly, she'd live.

And take whatever happened afterwards squarely on the chin. She wasn't like her mother, sadly believing that passion and love were the same.

Eyes narrowed against the sun, she watched him stride towards her, his lean, powerful body and fabulous face attracting plenty of attention, which he ignored. She felt the impact of his gaze on her, purposeful and definitely territorial, recharging her with a nervous, reckless energy.

Her heart began to throb—fast, heavy strokes in her chest—and she felt her mouth go dry. Every moment of her life until then had been preparation for this, as though without realising it she'd been waiting for him.

And while common sense wondered what she'd do if he was merely passing through the resort, a deeper, more basic instinct knew he'd come for her.

He stopped beside her and said, 'Giselle.'

Just one word, a name she'd heard thousands of times before, yet it told her everything.

Looking up into his dark, hard face, she said, 'It took you long enough.'

He sat down on the end of the lounger, examining her face with a formidable, relentless scrutiny that didn't hide the heat in his gaze. 'I had things to do.'

She nodded.

One black brow rose in sardonic appreciation. 'Is it so simple, then?'

'I think so.' The heady clamour of desire stripped away her inhibitions. 'Why make it any more complex?'

'An unusual attitude,' he said, his voice dropping several tones. 'But then you're an unusual woman. Have you missed me?'

Possibly all my life, she thought, but said aloud, 'As much as you've missed me, I imagine.'

He gave a taut, mirthless smile, and touched her knee. The gesture was fleeting, barely noticeable, yet it reverberated through every cell of her body in a fusion of excitement and anticipation.

She had to concentrate hard when he asked, 'Do you wish to stay here? The yacht is available, and we can be private there.'

Caution warred with an instinctive understanding that this man was trustworthy.

'No?' he said, divining her thoughts with unnerving

accuracy. 'I do not harm women, but you are wise not to take anyone on trust. Can I persuade you to come with me to a quieter resort, where you can be sure of your safety yet we will be more private?'

She met his eyes, and saw desire glitter there, a controlled kindling of hunger to match her own, and a basic, bone-deep honesty. He wasn't promising love, or tenderness, or anything more than the sating of a passion that had been gnawing at her ever since she'd seen him.

'What exactly do you have in mind?' she asked, testing him further.

'Anything that happens will be your decision.' His voice was deceptively cool.

He could afford to say that, because he knew that she wanted him as much as he did her. But, driven by the recklessness she hadn't known she possessed, she said evenly, 'I'll have to let my family know where I am.'

'Is there a problem with that?'

'No, I'll ring my—my aunt.' Aunt sounded more responsible than godmother, but the lie was difficult. And ringing Maura would probably eat up the last of her phone card.

She thought of Leola in London, then decided impetuously that it wouldn't hurt her sister to wait for four days to find out about Parirua. It wasn't as though she could do anything. 'Where are we going?'

'Flying Fish.'

She sucked in a breath. Flying Fish was a fabled place on the other coast, one that wasn't advertised anywhere but in supplements dedicated to the very rich who wanted the utmost discretion and privacy.

'Ring your aunt.' He got to his feet. 'I'll organise your leaving from here.'

'All right.'

'I think perhaps it will make you feel a little more safe if I do it, so that the management here knows where you are and who you are with.'

Although he couldn't have had much to do with nervous virgins, he knew how to soothe them. She said wryly, 'It's not that I don't trust you—'

'If I had a sister,' he said, choosing his words deliberately, 'I would make sure she knew how to protect herself. You are sensible, and I like that.'

Roman waited for her response. Most other women would have met his comment with a flirtatious glance and the hope that he liked other things about them too.

However, a small smile lifted the corners of her lush mouth. 'I don't think I'm being very sensible at all, but what the hell?' Her eyes blazed with green fire as she looked directly at him. 'Are *you* being sensible?'

She had no idea how much of a challenge she was. For some reason he wanted her beyond the usual casual desire, the urgent hunger of a virile man for an attractive woman. She could be a beauty; she simply didn't give a damn. Stripped like this to the basics—the sleek but somewhat elderly swimsuit showing off high, curved breasts, a narrow waist and those long, lithe legs—she was pure seduction. Add to that the combination of exquisite skin, barely tinged with a faint gold wash after her time in the Tropics, and sloe-shaped eyes, the strong, svelte lines and curves of her body—and, he admitted, the quick tongue and openness of her response to him—and he felt himself hardening.

'What has sense got to do with us?' And, because he was damned if he was going to kiss her there, with people covertly watching and commenting, he said curtly, 'Let's go.'

An hour later Giselle watched the water come up to meet the little amphibian plane, felt the slight jolt of its floats kiss the surface of the lagoon just as the sun slid beneath the limitless horizon, dusk crowding its heels.

The island Roman had brought her to was small, its central hills covered in thick jungle, the shores lined with the feathery fans of coconut palms bending to the turquoise lagoon. When the engines changed pitch to a roar and the plane ran up onto the sand, she thought with a catch to her breath that she'd well and truly burnt her boats.

Yet her heart sang with anticipation. Just this once she was going to live. It would be a jewel of memory to hold for ever, something to ease the pain of selling Parirua.

Roman helped her down onto gleaming white coral sand, still hot from the sun, and while someone from the resort took out their luggage and the manager greeted them sedately and with great respect, she thought, You've done it now. No going back...

Because although he'd said they could take it at her pace, she knew she had no resistance to him. Tonight she'd lie in his arms and learn what it was like to make love to him.

Side by side they walked up a sandy path to an airy bungalow built from native materials so that it blended into the thick, tropical undergrowth. Hibiscuses held their frilly cups up to the dying light of the sun, and to one side a huge tree sheltered a terrace.

'Welcome,' the manager said one last time, and left them to go inside by themselves.

It had been decorated beautifully, the soft colours highlighted by vivid splashes from the flowers that scented the air.

She said quietly, 'This is lovely.'

After a keen glance at her, Roman said, 'I think you need a drink. And for an occasion like this, there is only one thing to serve.'

Giselle had drunk champagne before, and enjoyed it, but

this, she thought, eyeing the bottle he took from the bar fridge, was going to be something else again. Although the label was in French, she recognised the name.

Of course he removed the cork with no fuss at all, and then poured two glasses, bringing one across to her. Giselle clung to the fragile flute so tightly she wondered if she might snap the stem. Surreptitiously she eased her grip and tried to look sophisticated.

Roman said, 'Shall we drink to courage? And to joy.'

Oddly touched by his coupling of the two words, she said, 'Yes, I'd like that.'

There had been very little joy in her life for a long time. No matter how much she tried, she knew she'd been a poor substitute for the son her father had wanted. Nobody could love Parirua more, or work harder for it, but it hadn't been enough.

And it had all been for nothing.

'To joy,' she said, lifting her glass. 'And to courage.'

The champagne was cool and delicious, slightly yeasty on her tongue; it tasted like heaven, she thought, and sipped again before putting the glass down on a table. She'd expected to be embarrassed; in fact, the thought of that had almost persuaded her to rescind her decision halfway through packing.

But she hadn't. Strangely, although she knew practically nothing about Roman, she felt almost at ease.

So when he said, 'I suggest we order dinner. We can eat at the restaurant, or here,' she replied instantly, without the need for thought.

'Here.'

Other people would destroy the fantasy she'd indulged in, where they were two ordinary people and she could meet him on equal terms. She didn't know why he wanted her, but he did; and here, alone with him, she could forget that he had a royal heritage going back centuries—that he moved in circles where wealth and birth and sophistication were taken for granted.

While she still had the courage, she said, 'I hope you're not…not expecting too much. I haven't ever done this before.'

Black brows drew together. 'Done what?' Roman asked quietly, but a raw note in his voice touched a nerve.

Nevertheless she met his narrowed gaze candidly. 'Made love,' she said, angry at the rush of blood the simple words brought to her skin.

'So you are virgin.'

It was impossible to gauge his reaction. 'Yes,' she said baldly.

He set his glass down and stood looking at her, his eyes burnished and impenetrable. Then he said on a taut, hard note, 'I do not seduce virgins.'

'Seduction wasn't what I had in mind,' she told him, trying to sound cool and pragmatic while a pulse beat high in her throat. 'Making love was. Seduction implies that one person uses their skills to overcome another's scruples or principles.'

He was watching her, his face impassive.

Gathering her courage, she finished, 'I don't expect this to lead to anything and I'm here because I want to be. I more or less told you that beside the pool.'

'And charmingly open I thought you,' he said thought-fully. 'Can I be sure you know what you're doing? I don't break hearts.'

CHAPTER FOUR

GISELLE gave an enigmatic smile. 'A heart needs to love before it can be broken. *I* don't believe in love at first sight, or even second sight,' she told him. 'We don't even know each other.'

'Are all New Zealand women as open and frank as you?'

She shrugged. 'I don't know.'

Roman said even more thoughtfully, 'Because, if so, it makes me envious of my cousins Alex and Marco, who both married New Zealanders. Look at me, Giselle.'

It was only the third time he'd said her name. Her heart shook inside her, but she raised her eyes, holding them steady when he came across and cupped her chin in his hand.

Tiny shivers of anticipation surged through her, and to her surprise he laughed, a soft, almost wondering sound. 'Yes, I think you do know what you're doing. Say my name.'

When she tried no noise emerged. He smiled at that, but she swallowed and tried again. 'Roman.'

'Rather like my old governess,' he said dryly.

He touched her lips with his finger, and against it she whispered, 'Roman.'

And he replaced the finger with his lips in a kiss so

gentle she barely felt it. Her lashes fluttered down and she began to slide her arms around him.

He took a step back, the heat in his eyes dispelling the chill that gripped her. 'Very well, then, let us be lovers, you and I. And just so that we are equal, I will tell you that this is a first for me, also. I have never made love to a virgin before.'

'Oh!' Colour flooded her face. 'So that makes us equal?' she said, her smile a little lopsided.

'I think so. Now, here is a menu for dinner. What would you like to eat?'

Numbly she accepted it from him, and sat down on the sofa to look at it. He joined her, casually slinging an arm across her shoulders, getting her accustomed, she thought, to his touch and his closeness—a bit like gentling a nervous horse.

'They do an interesting blend of tropical and Asian cooking here,' he said, 'and very sensibly use only local produce except for a few things that travel well.'

He was far too close, and she was so acutely aware of his hand on the bare skin of her shoulder that she had to concentrate on her breathing until the dancing letters of the menu settled down into words.

'*Poisson cru,*' she said, her voice husky. 'I've always loved it, so although I should try something I've never tasted before, I'll have that.'

When he didn't answer she looked up, to find that he wasn't examining the menu; instead his gaze was fixed on her face. She felt surrounded by him—by the faint, stimulating scent that was all male, by his arm and the width of his chest behind her, by the long, powerfully muscled thigh against hers. He overwhelmed her with the sheer force of his personality and his intense masculine strength.

Panic knotted deep in her belly, warring with another primal instinct—passion.

'I'll have *poisson cru* too,' he said.

He had a much better French accent than she did, she noticed. And because she was curious about him, she asked, 'How many languages do you speak?'

'Several.' He sounded surprised, but amused. 'English and French and Russian. Italian, and of course Illyrian. I can understand and make myself understood in German and Spanish and Mandarin, but I don't claim more than the bare competence in them.'

'Hugely cosmopolitan,' she said wryly. Somehow the list underlined the yawning gulf between his life and hers. She thrust that idea from her and went on, 'The only other language I know is Maori. My grandfather made the station hands talk to us only in that language. He spoke it, and he believed that every New Zealander should.'

'Is that your belief too?'

'Yes. It's native to New Zealand, and we should know it.'

He nodded. 'I agree. Now, what else would you like to eat?'

Her stomach tightened. She doubted whether she'd even be able to eat the fish marinated in coconut cream when it arrived; her nerves were already jumping, and although she had no intention of backing out, she found herself wondering feverishly if he'd find her boring and inadequate in bed.

Nevertheless she chose, letting out her breath in a slow sigh when he left her to place the order on the telephone. She needed space, so she picked up her glass and wandered across to the window. While they'd been talking the last of the sun's light had faded and the moon hadn't risen, so she could see nothing but the limitless darkness of night.

Although he moved silently, she knew when he approached her, and without volition she stiffened.

Her suspicion that he noticed was confirmed when he

said, 'Don't be afraid. There are two bedrooms here; all you have to do is say so, and we will sleep separately.'

She said quietly, 'I'm not afraid. Just—green.'

'Why did you decide on this?'

Because she was at a turning point in her life. And she couldn't help herself. He was the only man she'd ever wanted enough to forget about caution and take a chance. At some intimate, cellular level she knew that if she hadn't chosen him to be her first lover she'd have regretted it for the rest of her life.

It did occur to her that he might be her only lover, but she dismissed the thought as soon as it came. Nobody could foresee the future, and it was a waste of time second-guessing it.

His words echoed in her ears. *I don't break hearts*, he'd said, and he'd meant it. He had principles, and if he thought this was too important for her he might refuse.

So she said, 'Because I find you very attractive. You know that.'

'Of course—it was obvious from the moment our eyes met. But I'm sure you've found other men attractive. Although desire is a fierce force, it can be controlled.'

He was making sure she understood that he wasn't in love with her. Well, that was fine; she wasn't in love with him either.

Gaze skimming the darkened sea that gleamed in the star-shine like old pewter, she said, 'Isn't that—desire—enough?'

'Perhaps for any other woman, but I find it interesting that someone who has resolutely kept her virginity for what—twenty-four years...?'

'Spot on,' she said briefly. Oh, he knew a lot about women to be able to pinpoint her age so accurately.

'...should decide suddenly to rid herself of it.'

Giselle swung around and looked up into his autocratic face, its magnificent bone structure and disciplined, sensuous mouth disturbingly taut. 'Do you want me to tell you that you're the most attractive man I've ever met?'

Amazed, she saw colour highlight the slash of his cheekbones. She felt almost light-headed, dizzy with pleasure at having startled him. 'Why are you surprised? You must know you're very good-looking.'

Hooded eyes glinting, he shrugged. 'It's been said before—in fact, when I started out in business it was a distinct asset,' he admitted. 'People tend to think that a handsome face means there can only be fluff behind it, so they underestimated me.'

'Only superficial people,' she observed, wondering how anyone could make the mistake of thinking that because he looked like something exotic out of a Mediterranean drama he lacked strength.

His smile was edged. 'I find your frankness almost shocking. But the combination of genes that blessed my birth doesn't necessarily mean that you can trust me.'

'I know that,' she said immediately, wondering how she could talk so frankly to him. 'But you've been as honest with me as I've been with you. I told you I didn't have time or space in my life for a relationship, and it's true. I don't expect anything from you, and once we leave here I'll never see you again. There's something I should have asked, though, and didn't. Are you in any sort of relationship?'

'No,' he said crisply.

Stifling a huge relief, she said, 'The woman on the beach…?'

'No.' This time on an uncompromising note.

Compelled to force the issue, she said, 'She wanted it.'

Again he shrugged, more deeply this time, his eyes

holding hers in an uncomfortably direct manner, as though probing for her innermost secrets. 'Perhaps. But there was nothing between us.' And before she could say anything he asked, 'Would it have bothered you?'

'I…yes,' she admitted. 'Yes, it would have.'

'You need not worry. I am not promiscuous.'

Her brows climbed as she thought of the A-list of beauties who'd been his lovers.

Roman's mouth hardened. 'You shouldn't believe gossip,' he said indifferently. 'Most of it is written to sell newspapers and magazines.'

Obscurely comforted by his statement, she nodded. 'I know that.'

'Anyone with a title—no matter how old or defunct—can expect more than their fair share of comment and downright lies.'

Which explained his reaction when he'd caught her spying, as he'd believed. And his suggestion that they leave the other resort.

Eerily echoing her thoughts, he said, 'Did you manage to contact your family?'

'Yes.' Though she'd been guiltily glad that she'd had to leave a message on her godmother's answering machine; she hadn't looked forward to the explanations.

Not that Maura would have protested. Actually, she'd have probably cheered her on, but somehow these days with Roman were too precious to share with anyone else.

'So,' Roman said, picking up his glass, 'tell me what you want to do while you are here.' He ignored the colour that stole into her skin and went on, 'If you wish me to organise activities we can do that—there is an excellent diving instructor here—but if you prefer to lie on the beach that is fine too. We have a private cove and won't be disturbed.'

'I have to be careful about sunbathing,' she told him, adding enviously, 'You're so lucky to have olive skin. Mine won't tan.'

'Why would you want it to? It is exquisite as it is.'

His voice was calm and noncommittal, but tension hummed between them, an awareness that simmered just beneath the surface. She felt truly alive, as though until then she'd been sleepwalking through life, unaware of anything but the mundane.

That was when she realised, with a kind of desperate apprehension, that her life was never going to be the same again. No matter what happened, she would be completely changed by meeting Roman Magnati.

So enjoy it, she told herself, and took another, slightly larger sip of champagne. 'Thank you. Shall we just see how things pan out?' she suggested.

He nodded, turning before she realised that someone was approaching. It was the waiter with the first course of their dinner; a tall, solemn islander, he acknowledged Roman's greeting with a sedate smile, and set the table, then put out the dishes for the entrée, lit candles, and left.

'You must come here often to know the staff by their names,' Giselle said.

The prince seated her and sat down opposite. 'He wants to go into the hospitality business so he's starting from the bottom up. The resort is run by the local villagers, and any who wish to do more than wait or clean or keep the visitors entertained have the opportunity to go further.'

'Do you own this place?' she asked.

'In conjunction with the villagers,' he said coolly. 'Does it matter?'

'No, of course not. Similar ventures are working well at home. I just didn't think that…' she hesitated; *foreign-*

ers sounded such a nasty word '…that people from out of the area got involved in such things.'

'I'm interested in this sort of development, and if I'm to be of any use to the people in Illyria who seem to look to me for help, I need to know how such things work and any pitfalls.'

Giselle had hoped he wouldn't feel obliged to woo her. She didn't want fake romance. Neither did he, apparently; while they ate the meal they talked as equals about his hopes and plans for the land he'd never seen until a few years ago.

And when they'd finished a tongue-tingling dessert of tropical fruit he said, 'Would you like to go for a walk? The view from the top of the hill is superb, and no doubt you can tell me the names of the Southern Hemisphere constellations.'

'Some of them,' she said cautiously.

The path up the hill was lit by small golden lamps that came on as they approached and died once they'd passed.

'Solar powered,' Roman said when she commented on them. 'Like most of the island.'

The view spread out below them; Giselle turned slowly, checking out the white line of the reef, irregular around the island. On the lagoon, clusters of lights gathered and separated before coalescing again like swarms of fireflies.

She asked, 'What are they doing?'

'Catching fish for tomorrow night's dinner,' he said.

The smile in his tone made her say, 'It looks so *romantic*!'

And immediately regretted it.

'Romance is where you find it,' he said, adding with a smile, 'Our chef would almost certainly say that good fish is very romantic.'

'I'd agree with him,' she said thoughtfully. 'That *poisson cru* was ambrosia.'

She began to point out the various stars and constellations, giving him the Maori names and legends for each, saying when at last she ran out, 'They look so close. I thought nothing could be as beautiful as the night sky at home, but this is extraordinary.'

'So,' he said steadily, 'are you.'

He touched her shoulder. She froze, but after a second she sighed and turned into his arms and lifted her face, her body poised and clamorous with heat, her whole attention on him. His expression was fierce and a little predatory, his eyes narrowed and intent.

Later, she couldn't recall what she'd done to make his hands on her arms clench, but by the time he pulled her into the lean, hard warmth of his body he was already fully aroused.

He said her name against her lips, and then crushed it into oblivion, taking his fill of her in a way that should have satisfied some of the wildfire need pounding through her. It didn't. Instead, the kiss fuelled it, sending her up in flames, scorching through her inhibitions and inchoate fears and the veneer of worldliness she'd pulled around her over the past twenty-four hours.

When she shivered, Roman said on an abrasive note, 'Let's go back.'

'Yes,' she said simply.

But she ached with emptiness when he released her, an emptiness only partly relieved by his hand at her elbow as they headed down the path towards the cabin.

Neither spoke. The silence between them was fraught with tension, a force that linked them yet somehow divided them.

Back inside she looked into Roman's face, her heart jumping at the fierce hunter's concentration honing his features. While they'd been gone the remnants of the dinner had been cleared away and the lights dimmed so that the room was sultry with shadows and the glow of several lamps.

Roman reached for the clip she used to keep her hair back from her face, freeing the crimson flower she'd tucked into it. Her hair fell in a silken cloud around her face.

He held the flower to his nose, and when she said, 'Hibiscuses have no scent,' he smiled.

'You're wrong. It smells of you,' he told her. 'Warm, candid, vital—and like you it's touched with mystery. Look at the heart of it—the darkest, most saturated red I've ever seen. You have an instinctive touch for what is befitting; that colour shows up your midnight glamour.'

Heat flooded her skin. 'You don't have to—I'm not at all—'

He stopped the words with a finger across her lips. 'Lady, you so *are*,' he said, the words deep and sure and raw. He bent his head before she could say any more and kissed the objection from her lips, and her protests fled under the ravishing eroticism of his touch.

Thoughts tangled in her mind, then floated off, borne in a tide of delicious sensations. She opened her mouth to his, quivering at her unlimited response to his deep, deep kisses, at the eager hunger that tightened inside her and cried out for appeasement, for satiation. Her lashes fluttered down; helplessly she yielded to the potent enchantment of passion.

When he lifted his head she opened her eyes, her questioning gaze held by the gathering storm in his. 'You are beautiful,' he rasped.

Against his mouth she whispered, 'So are you.'

He laughed in his throat. 'Then touch me, Giselle…'

At her startled glance his mouth twisted with wry humour. 'Both of us are in this, my sweet girl. We kiss, we touch, we make love together. Aren't you curious about the way I feel? Don't you want to run your hands across my shoulders—like this?'

His hands slid up to cup her neck; she trembled at the slightly roughened skin of his fingers as his thumbs stroked slowly over the vulnerable hollow in her throat. He gave a narrow smile at the leap of her pulse beneath his fingers, before letting them drift to the back of her neck.

She'd never known that the skin there was acutely sensitive; his slow caress sent shivers of excitement scudding down her spine, arrowing into the pit of her belly. 'Yes,' she whispered, unable to remember what she was answering.

His smile taut, he measured the width of her shoulders, his touch seeking, gentle, yet making himself master of her responses.

'So,' he said softly. 'Try it.'

She lifted shaking hands, and undid the buttons down the front of his shirt, parting the warm material to reveal the sleek, tanned skin beneath. He stilled, his hands resting loosely on her upper arms. Tentatively, hardly daring to breathe, she pushed the shirt back. He was big, she thought in wonder; a tall woman herself, she hadn't realised how much pure, compelling power was encased in his lean body until the muscles in his shoulder stood out as she touched the skin there with a light, barely discernible finger.

An electric shock ran through her. She gasped, and looked up into eyes that were wholly dark except for glittering blue sparks in their depths.

Dazedly she accepted that the tense muscles along his jaw and beneath her finger meant Roman was just as affected by her shy, amateur caress as she was; the knowledge emboldened her to press the palm of her hand against him, absorbing some of his strength. She leaned forward and breathed in his scent, a faint, unbearably exciting mixture of salt and musk, then kissed the place her hand had been.

She felt his heart kick into double time against her lips, and he said hoarsely, 'You see, it works both ways.'

And he bent his head. She thought he was going to kiss her, and held her face up, but his mouth landed on the juncture of neck and shoulders, and instead of a kiss he bit—almost tenderly, his teeth grazing her skin with just enough force to send violent rills of sensation shivering through her. Her knees shook, and she clung to him with hands that barely held her upright.

'I think we had better move from here.' His voice was harsh and flat.

Alarmed, she looked up, met eyes that were hooded and stripped of everything but blazing hunger. He kissed her, swift and fierce, then she gasped as he swung her up in his arms and carried her through the door and into the big main bedroom.

He deposited her on the bed and looked down at her. Giselle struggled with a sudden awareness of being smaller than he was, and a disconcerting feeling of fragility. The strength she'd always been rather proud of seemed very minor now.

Several quick movements shucked off his shirt; he came down beside her, sitting on the edge of the bed and disconcerted her by asking, 'Better?'

Eyes enormous in her face, she nodded.

He said seriously, 'I won't hurt you. Oh, perhaps a little when it happens, but only then. Do you understand that?'

How had he read her mind so easily? 'Yes,' she said in a muted voice. 'Sorry.'

'You will not say so again. Women have every right to be careful; they are vulnerable when making love.' He held her gaze. 'Perhaps the only greater time is during pregnancy and labour.'

She flushed, and he said swiftly, 'It's all right. I'll make sure there will be no pregnancy for us.'

The swift pang of regret bewildered her; she lay still and quiet, and he bent and kissed her again, and that odd little sorrow vanished under a rekindled surge of passionate desire.

'So, I need to dispose of this pretty thing,' he said, and skilfully unwrapped her sarong, spreading the cotton out on either side in a wash of colour. 'You look like a pearl in a crimson rose,' he said quietly.

And he kissed first one peaking nipple, and then the other. Sensation so intense it made Giselle gasp lifted her hips from the bed in a startling, involuntary movement. She pressed her thighs together, trying to contain the exquisite rush of arousal, but it left her quivering and with hands clenched on the sarong.

'What do you want?' he asked against the soft curve of her breast.

The movement of his mouth summoned a fresh goad to her anticipation. 'You,' she said in a hoarse, agitated voice. 'I want you.'

'And you shall have me, but not just yet. You are not yet ready.'

Not yet ready? If she were any more ready she'd explode in a firestorm of sensation, she thought wildly. Her whole body was aching with desperation, every cell tight with a kind of glorious expectation. She watched with slumbrous eyes as he divested himself of his trousers, her heart racing at the sight of him, all power and potent male grace.

Possibly she should have been startled—even scared— by how very aroused he was, but something primitive and untamed in her rejoiced, and when he came down beside her she turned to him and looped her arm around his hips and pulled herself against him.

This is where I am meant to be, she thought.

Roman said on a strained note, 'Not yet, my lovely one. Not just yet.'

But she had felt the leap of his flesh as they'd touched, and she knew he wanted her with a hunger that met and matched hers.

She said, 'Then what?'

'This,' he said, and bent to kiss her breast again, and take the urgent, pleading tip into his mouth.

CHAPTER FIVE

IN THAT instant Giselle lost all sense of time, all understanding of the world outside this bed, this man, the crimson
pareu beneath them. Roman's mouth burned away everything but the hunger to know him in the deepest, most
intimate way, to abandon herself to a rapture she'd never
imagined could be possible.

At first timidly and then with more confidence, she
explored his body as he explored hers, her fingertips
tingling with excitement when she traced the scroll of hair
across his chest and down his flat belly, until his hand
covered hers and eased it away.

'Not just yet,' he said on a low, husky laugh. 'You have
too much effect on me for that. Later.'

She pouted, but he slid his fingers into her, and the pout
was transformed into a choking gasp, and once more her
hips arced off the erotic warmth of the sarong and thrust
against his hand.

Violent pleasure rioted through her; she groaned his name.

'Soon,' he promised, but he pulled back and sat up.

Chilled, her confidence draining away, she frowned,
only to relax when she saw what he was doing—making
sure there'd be no unwanted results from this wild passion.

Again that intense regret ached through her; at that moment she'd have given her heart's blood to be able to say, 'Don't worry about it.'

But she'd bitterly repent it, and he wouldn't take any notice; he didn't want a child any more than she did.

That hurt in some core part of her, and the smile she gave him when he came back to her was tremulous.

'I'm ready,' she said quietly, desperate to lose herself in the rapture his touch promised.

He pierced her with a look, then bent his head to take her mouth in a kiss so potently seductive she thought she felt her heart leave her chest. His mouth was hot and masterful, drugging her with its promise of unslaked desire. Frantically she twisted beneath him, and he lifted his head and looked at her, his eyes narrowed and glittering as he took her with one strong thrust, lodging himself so far inside her that her body stiffened, her lashes flying wide.

'You are all right?' he demanded roughly. 'Did I hurt you?'

She muttered, 'No. Not at all—it just feels…strange. As though I've been taken over. But very all right—more all right than I've ever been.'

'Good. And I have not taken you over—this is a mutual thing between us.'

His smile was strangely tender. Again he thrust, and a shock of rapture startled her into an answering movement of her hips, a claim that came from some mysterious female part of her. Her hands skidded over his damp shoulders; she relished the coil and bunch of his muscles beneath her fingertips with a primal intensity that stoked every physical sensation.

Exulting in his forceful masculinity and her own feminine power, she followed his lead and together they set up a rhythm of advance and retreat, of slow, sensuous, achingly frustrating sensations that built and built and built until her whole body was a conduit for more pleasure than she could bear...

And then he thrust hard and fast, and she imploded, tossed higher and higher in waves of rapture until the final one overwhelmed her and she soared, only to be pushed further when he followed her into that unknown place where nothing but their physical communion meant anything any more.

As the keen, desperate ecstasy faded into delicious satiation, she wondered dreamily if she had been made for this, to lie beneath him and feel his arms around her, his weight pressing her into the bed, so happy that she thought she might never want to find the real world again.

After a few seconds he rolled over, carrying her with him. Still locked together, they lay side by side. Giselle felt dazed, disconnected, looking back on the woman she'd been—a woman who'd never known such ecstatic fulfilment—with a kind of tolerant sadness.

'You are not hurt?' Roman asked, his voice almost abrupt.

When she shook her head against the firm bulge of his shoulder, he turned her face to meet his eyes. Colour heated her skin, but she met his gaze fearlessly.

After few seconds of examination he smiled. 'Sweet voluptuary,' he said in a low purr that sent tiny shivers of renewed pleasure through her as he buried his face in the flying silk of her hair on the pillow.

Smiling, she kissed his shoulder. His skin was sleek and supple above the hard strength of his body, and when she licked the place she'd kissed his breathing altered, became swift and heavy.

Hugely content with the world, she expanded, 'It was pure pleasure all the way through.' She licked her lips, and tasted his sweat on them. A swift sharp thrill took her by surprise. 'Thank you. I hope it was good for you.'

'Good is a meaningless word,' he said. 'It was—beyond special.'

Roman listened to the beat of his heart subside and thought ironically that she continually surprised him with her frankness, her refusal to play games as so many other women did, her calm self-assurance.

And now she'd done it once more, with her simple, sincere thanks.

As well, she was having the most amazing effect on him. At the touch of her mouth on his skin his body had stirred and he desired her again, so fiercely it made him wonder whether she was some sort of ferociously addictive drug. Her lithe, curved body lay relaxed against him, the translucent skin already losing the flush his love-making had engendered.

He wanted to take her again and again, feel the smooth skin beneath his hands, the heat of her body, hear those choked little gasps as she climaxed beneath and around him.

It was impossible; she might not have felt any pain, but she wasn't used to the exercise and she'd probably be sore.

He had passionately hungered for other women, but always he'd been able to leash his natural male libido. This was different, and he didn't like it. It made him feel oddly vulnerable.

It took all his self-control to say calmly, 'Do you want to shower?'

Giselle wanted nothing more than to stay locked in his arms, but perhaps she was embarrassing him with her open gratitude. It certainly wasn't a sophisticated way to behave, she thought with a pang, remembering those other women he'd been linked with, who probably took their orgasms for granted.

Falsely bright, she said, 'Yes, that would be wonderful.'

The main bathroom was sparsely opulent, its tropical combination of white walls and dark timber lightened by a fern in the corner and the voluptuous scent of frangipani seeping in through the shutters. She'd wondered if he might want to shower with her, but he used the other bathroom.

They met again in the living room, she clad in another pareu—this one in wild swirls of charcoal and cyclamen and plum—he with a swathe of white around his lean hips. Her heart thudded at the return of that sweet, drugged languor.

So when he said, 'Do you prefer to sleep alone?' it came almost as a slap in the face.

'I don't know,' she said. 'I've never slept with anyone.'

He gave her a gleaming smile, narrow and taut. 'Then you should at least try it,' he suggested.

So they did. At first she lay there stiffly, but he was clearly accustomed to sharing a bed. He kissed her lightly, then not quite so lightly, before settling back against the pillows.

'Go to sleep,' he said, and to her astonishment she did, cloaked in security—another thing she'd never experienced.

Looking back, Giselle thought that Roman gave her the complete fantasy, a tropical idyll that would stay lodged in her mind for ever. During the next three days he was everything a woman could desire—tender, thoughtful, fascinating, completely attentive. He made her laugh, he kept her in a constant, delicious state of arousal, and made love to her with the skill and rapacity of a tender conqueror.

To be sure, she knew she was seeing only part of him. Every day for an hour he closeted himself with his telephone and his laptop and worked, and even when that was done she was aware that he kept most of his formidable self locked away.

Oh, he was hugely interesting; they talked about everything, and he made her think as she hadn't done before. She asked him once where he'd gone to university, and when he told her she nodded thoughtfully. 'An excellent institution.'

And very select in its choice of students. Clearly he was brilliant.

'How about you?' he asked.

She shrugged. 'I went from school to working on the farm.'

'Why?'

Because she loved Parirua. And because her father needed someone to look after him.

Not that he'd said so. He was never an openly affectionate man, she'd wondered if half the time he even realised she was there.

But he'd been driving himself into the ground, working too hard, drinking and smoking too much. When he'd developed a bad case of bronchitis during the twins' last year at boarding school she'd made the not-difficult decision to join him at Parirua and try to fill some of the emptiness of his life. She'd failed.

Hastily she finished, 'I have no talents, no burning desire to do anything else, so it was logical for me to stay there and do what I could to help.'

Eyes half closed, he leaned back in his chair and looked at her. 'Oh, I wouldn't say you have no talents,' he said softly. And as colour stung her cheeks he added with a smile, 'Does working on the station satisfy you?'

'I love the place.' Her heart contracted, because soon she'd have to leave it. She'd always hoped that one day she'd meet a man who'd love Parirua as much as she did, but that wasn't going to happen now.

She banished the gloomy thought. Live for the

present, she told herself with tough realism. Enjoy each day as it comes.

'That is not an answer to my question.'

Made uneasy by his refusal to let her evade the issue, she shrugged again and met his penetrating gaze with a limpid glance. 'Most farmers find their lives extremely satisfying.'

'Does your mother approve of your choice?'

'My mother is dead,' she told him without any emotion, her tone daring him to probe further.

He accepted that, smoothly changing the subject. A few minutes later his cell phone rang. 'Excuse me,' he said, and got to his feet, walking away from her as he spoke into it.

For some reason that hurt, but she was getting much better at pushing her reactions to the back of her mind. She had no right to resent the way he slotted her into a compartment that had nothing to do with the rest of his life; after all, she was doing exactly the same with him. They had laid out their terms. Roman's world of high finance and power and money, of bloodlines reaching back into antiquity, didn't have any place for her.

Anyway, she didn't want to be part of it. The mere thought of it frightened her—partly because soon it would take him away from her, leaving her with only memories.

But what memories! When they made love Roman held nothing back, using his magnificent body to wring an ecstatic release from her over and over again until she felt imprinted by him, so familiar with the touch and feel of him that she could have sculpted him from clay.

And he seemed to find an equal delight in her. Slowly, imperceptibly, she had learned that she could dazzle him as he did her, that he wasn't lying when he praised her silken skin and her strength, her green eyes and the long tangle of her black hair. For the first time in her life, she felt cherished.

She'd fought against weakly succumbing to that knowledge, knowing that to accept it—worse, to let herself come to rely on it—was a danger to any hopes of happiness she might ever have.

Concentrate on enjoying what you've got, she told herself for possibly the fiftieth time, looking up expectantly as he came back.

Something had happened. His expression was closed, his handsome face hard and remote, his eyes hooded against her.

Chilled, she braced herself.

'I'm afraid I have to leave you in the morning,' he said, his voice curt and uninflected. 'I'm needed.'

He was lying. She didn't know how she knew it, but she did. This, she thought, an icy hollow forming beneath her ribs, was how a prince cast off a temporary mistress. A roiling anguish took her by surprise; she realised with a flare of panic that a future without Roman was empty and grey, devoid of everything that had made her so happy these past few days.

Was this how her mother had felt when she'd contemplated her life after she'd been abandoned by her lover?

Pride wouldn't let him see how much this swift, cutting rejection hurt and shocked her. She got to her feet. 'Is there anything I can do?'

'No. Of course you must see out the rest of your holiday here.' His automatic courtesy set a barrier between them.

'Thank you,' she said numbly, making up her mind to leave as soon as he was safely gone. Almost she wished he'd tell her why he'd lied, but bad news had no part in this tropical idyll.

Besides, if this was something to do with his business, he wouldn't tell her.

She straightened her shoulders, meeting his burnished, unreadable eyes with a slight lift of her chin.

Still with that chilling courtesy he said, 'I'll sleep in the other room. I have to leave early, and I don't want to wake you.'

After a frozen second, she said numbly, 'Of course.'

Not that she slept. All night she fought against creeping into his bedroom and seducing him; it took every particle of steely self-control to keep her in the bed they'd shared.

And when he rose before the sun had risen above the reef, she lay and listened for him to come to her.

In the end, she got up and dressed in the pareu she'd worn to the Island Night. As she walked out into the living room she heard a helicopter flying low from the mainland.

Roman was dressed in more formal clothes than she'd ever seen, and somehow the cool tropical suit underlined the distance between them.

He looked up when she said, 'Safe journey, Roman.'

'I'd hoped not to wake you,' he said, and took both her hands, kissing one palm then the other.

He held them for a moment, his midnight eyes searching her face before he leaned down and kissed her mouth, quite gently at first, and then—when her mouth moulded to his—with a swift, shattering passion that tore at her heartstrings.

He stopped it immediately. 'I didn't intend that,' he said harshly.

'Goodbye.' Her voice hid the impassioned grief that tore at her composure. 'And...thank you.'

'There is no need.' Arrogant features formidably impassive, he stepped back. In a tone and phraseology that made him no longer the lover but the prince, he said, 'If anyone should be grateful, it is I. I have enjoyed these past days very much.'

He didn't ask her to go down to the beach with him, and she didn't offer. Her composure was brittle enough to shatter; she didn't want him to realise how close she was to breaking down and bawling her eyes out.

Tears stung as she watched the chopper rising into a soft, tropical sky tinged with the rosy fireworks of dawn. It must make life so simple, she thought, when you had power and vast amounts of money.

She'd never see him again.

Get over it, she told herself staunchly. It was wonderful and now it's finished, and that's that. Now you have to go home and sell Parirua. And then you have to find something to do with your life—preferably a job that doesn't involve serving behind the counter in a fast-food restaurant. Roman has gone, but you still have Leola and Maura.

When her cell phone warbled in the shiny minimalist foyer of the Auckland high-rise building, Giselle groped for it and turned blindly to the wall. 'Hello?'

Leola sounded worried. 'Ellie, is it done?'

'Yes.' If she let the tiniest bit of emotion leak through she'd shatter and end up bawling like a baby. 'Everything's signed; Parirua isn't ours any more.'

'I wish I could be there,' Leola said wearily, 'but I can't—*daren't*—ask for time off.'

'I know. Don't worry, I'm fine.'

'Come off it! I *know* how much you're going to miss it.'

'Lollie, don't. It had to be done.'

Fortunately the organisation she'd derisively nicknamed MegaCorp had still been eager to buy the station at a price that would pay the taxes and the penalties and even leave a small—a very small—amount over to be shared between the two sisters.

Her sister said urgently, 'What happens now?'

Giselle forced her voice into an unnatural steadiness. 'I'm to manage it for six months. Joe and Rangi stay on too. The money's in the bank, and I've just posted a cheque to the Inland Revenue.'

'What are you planning to do right now?' Her twin's voice sharpened. 'Not drive back home, I hope?'

'No, I'm staying at Maura's.'

'Good. I don't think you should be alone.'

Giselle didn't intend to let her sister know that Maura was in Australia. 'I'm not going to disintegrate.'

'Of course you're not, but there's something going on that I don't understand—I can hear it in your voice. Tell me that you met someone nice on Fala'isi.'

Nice? Giselle's smile was a blend of loss and fortitude. Instead she reiterated, 'I'm fine.'

'You did! Tell me about him!'

To cheer her up, Giselle yielded. 'Well, actually I met someone, but it's not what you think.' She recounted her first meeting with Roman, making it a joke.

Leola didn't laugh. Almost uncertainly she said, 'Actually, I've met the Lord of the Sea Isles. What did you think of him?'

Some note—of withdrawal, or pain?—in her sister's voice snapped Giselle's instincts into high alert. Was it possible she'd been wrong—that it had been Leola in the photograph? Oh, why had she thrown it away?

'Dishy,' she said succinctly, wishing she'd kept silent. 'What about you?'

'Likewise. But I've always been a sucker for a killer smile, and a look that says *Don't even think of messing with me*,' Leola laughed, shaking off whatever had altered her tone. 'And we're not alone—even princesses fight to get within touching distance. Did you like him?'

'*Like* isn't exactly the term I'd use,' Giselle said scrupulously.

Her twin's gurgle of laughter sounded strained. 'Overwhelmed you a bit, did he?'

'A bit,' she said honestly, hoping that nothing of her stark misery showed in her tone.

'They're an overwhelming family.' Leola paused, then went on airily, 'Remember watching Prince Alex's coronation on the news years ago?'

'Yes. Yes, I do.' Giselle had been impressed at the Illyrians' single-minded determination to set their hereditary ruler on the throne, whether he wanted to be there or not.

'It was so—so hugely, dramatically symbolic and magical and strange—all of those miserable, hungry-looking people in their drab clothes and shaggy hair just snatching him up and carrying him off to the cathedral and crowning him.' Leola sighed. 'And last year his three cousins got married in that same cathedral. Apart from the drama of a triple wedding, the clothes were fabulous!'

Leola sounded perfectly normal, but Giselle knew her twin too well. She was avoiding something. Perhaps the sale of Parirua was affecting her more than she'd admit.

The alternative—that her sister had fallen for Roman—was too bizarre to contemplate. Coincidences were one thing, but that—that would be beyond belief.

Her thoughts were interrupted by her sister's voice. 'I'd better go. Keep smiling, Ellie.'

'I will.' Quickly Giselle said goodbye, hoping as she dropped her cell phone back in her bag that she'd convinced her that all was well.

She stared around, and shivered, thinking she never wanted to see this place again, with its stark black furniture and hard, shiny marble, its manicured pot-plants and carefully chosen, innocuous art. She blew her nose fiercely and headed for the doors, but the stupid tears kept coming as she walked quickly out into the street.

From behind a voice said, 'Giselle.'

And her bleak misery evaporated, blown away by a joy so extreme she couldn't breathe. Disbelieving the evidence of her ears, she turned and saw him, magnificently clothed in a sombre business suit that made him seem even taller and more compelling than ever.

'Roman,' she said, her breath locking in her throat. 'What are you doing here?'

'Business and some pleasure.' He scanned her face, his eyes narrowing. 'You are upset.'

Automatically she said, 'No, I'm fine.' Fine? What a ridiculous word! Now that he was here she felt *wonderful*.

One brow lifted in irony. 'You're pale, and you don't look as though you've been sleeping well. Come in here and I'll get you a drink.' He took her elbow to steer her through a door into a hushed silence and dim luxury.

Short of an undignified struggle, she had no option. And she suddenly felt very odd indeed. Fainting would be the ultimate embarrassment. 'We seem to have had this conversation before,' she managed.

'Have you been drinking enough?'

She said vaguely, 'I had some coffee.'

Roman's firm grip on her elbow didn't relax until she was seated at a table some distance from the bar, almost hidden by a large bookshelf and a table with a huge urn of flowers.

But when a brandy arrived she said, 'No—I'd better have water.'

'And a sandwich, I think.'

Roman said something to the waitress and they sat in what rapidly became an awkward silence until the woman's return with a glass of chilled water. Awkward for Giselle, anyway; a fleeting glance at the man opposite found no sign of any emotion in his hard, handsome features. She couldn't read anything in his eyes, either.

'Sip it slowly,' Roman ordered.

At least he didn't probe. Giselle drew in a shuddering breath, then began to drink, aware of his gaze on her, remote yet penetrating. A few minutes later a sandwich appeared. Although the prospect of eating made her stomach churn, she picked up the food and slowly, carefully, forced it down, her skin prickling at the impact of his remote, relentless survey. From beneath her lashes she could see his suit, a dark, superbly cut one that sheathed his powerful body and his long legs with sophisticated authority.

And he was right, damn him. The sandwich settled her stomach, and the coffee that followed it gave her enough energy to wonder what on earth he was doing here.

He waited until she'd finished to say, 'What has happened to you?'

She was not going to discuss Parirua with him. 'I missed lunch.' Her voice sounded strange—distant and brittle and thin.

She made the mistake of lifting her lashes, and met eyes that were still opaque and more than a little intimidating.

Without expression, he said, 'You have a little more colour now.'

'I feel more like myself.' She looked around, realising how very out of place she was in this formal, comfortable bar, with its leather armchairs worn from a century of use, its elegant women and confident men.

Old money…

In spite of the continental cut of his suit and his aura of power, Roman Magnati fitted in far better than she did, yet once her family had been old money. Not as old as his, though.

Bella Adams' glamorous face danced in front of her eyes. The model had left her husband, and the media were full of speculation about the reasons for the split—gossip in which Roman's name figured quite largely, although always carefully phrased, presumably so that he couldn't sue.

Giselle said stiffly, 'I'm ready to go now. Thank you for being so kind.'

Her words produced a shrug of those broad shoulders. 'It was nothing,' he said, and got to his feet as she rose.

She'd forgotten how tall he was, how weak and ineffectual he could make her feel. She almost faltered when his hand gripped her elbow again.

'I'm quite able to walk by myself, thank you,' she said, rigidly controlling her voice because the feel of his fingers on her bare skin sent volcanic tremors through her.

He didn't let go. 'Perhaps,' he said, his faint accent colouring the word. 'But I'll take you wherever you're going.'

'I don't need an escort.'

'I think you do, and if that irritates your prickly pride I'm sorry.' Exasperation underlined his next words. 'Do you realise this is word for word a repetition of the Island Night on Fala'isi? I was brought up to be protective of women. And yes, I know you are strong and independent, but you are still too pale. Have you been ill?'

'No,' she said firmly.

'Where are you staying?'

'On the North Shore,' she said, adding with a snap, 'If you keep repeating the same actions, you're going to get the same reaction. On Fala'isi I didn't need to be cosseted, and I don't now. I'm sorry I seem a bit pale and wan, but I'm perfectly capable of taking care of myself.'

He frowned. 'I have an appointment in half an hour, so instead of taking you home I'll take you to my hotel, where you can rest until you feel better.'

Oddly touched, she said again, 'Roman, it's all right. *I'm* all right. And I don't want to go to your hotel.'

'In that case, I'll have to miss my appointment,' he said negligently, and smiled at her frustrated face.

It was difficult to meet his eyes, but Giselle did. 'There's no need for that,' she said between her teeth.

'I think there is.' His eyes were unreadable, but she saw the determination in his face, heard it in the edge to his voice as he went on, 'And as you insist you're fine, does that mean you'll be able to come out with me tonight?'

Giselle's breath stopped in her throat. A great surge of hope shocked her. 'Why?' she asked baldly.

He smiled down at her, his eyes narrowed and amused. 'Guess,' he invited.

Pain and sore pride and an aching heart goaded her into rudeness. 'Because taking me out is easier than finding a woman for the night?'

CHAPTER SIX

ROMAN looked down at her, his handsome face impassive. 'No,' he said quite pleasantly. 'And I resent the implication.'

Giselle bit her lip. 'It wasn't an implication,' she admitted, humiliated by the hurt that had driven that stupid response. 'I came right out and said it, and I'm sorry. It was uncalled for.'

'Then you can apologise in the best way by coming with me to this party tonight.'

Shamed anew, she said, 'I don't have any clothes suitable for the sort of occasion you'll be going to.'

'Then wear what you have. Or tell me that you don't want to come out with me.' Again his tone was even and neutral, but she heard the thread of steel through each word.

She cast him a withering look, furious at the way he made her feel, knowing that he read her reactions. He smiled, and leaned forward and took one of her hands, holding it loosely.

That was when she realised that she loved him, and that it wasn't going to go away. Panic rioted through her, and sheer, glorious wonder, and a sense of utter rightness, strong enough to strip her of words.

'Giselle,' he said gently, his gaze holding hers, 'if you

find me dull or boring tell me and I'll go—once I've delivered you to wherever you're staying.'

'You know perfectly well that I don't find you dull or boring,' she muttered.

'So what is your problem?' His fingers tightened a little around her hand. 'I'm sorry I didn't contact you after I left Flying Fish, but there was a reason—'

'It's all right,' she broke in desperately. She didn't want excuses, even if they were legitimate.

Roman frowned. 'I wish to explain—'

'Look, you don't owe me anything.' She drew in a breath and continued in her most decisive tone, 'We made a bargain on Fala'isi, and it still holds as far as I'm concerned. No strings, no claim.'

If she said *I'm in love with you*, she thought mordantly, it would probably get him out of her life fast and finally. And although that would eventually happen anyway, it was too dangerous to let herself sink further and further into love.

His eyes narrowed a fraction, but after a second's pause he said evenly, 'Very well, then. Tell me why you don't want to go out with me.'

I do want to go out with you, I do, but it would break my heart.

Knowing that she was in danger of falling in love with him changed everything. Because Parirua was no longer her responsibility she felt rootless, adrift yet oddly free. Although she'd planned to go back home tomorrow—and she'd still do that—she'd allow herself a final night with Roman.

And then she'd go back to Parirua for six months and heal herself of this doomed love with more hard work. At least when she slogged all day she could sleep at night, and under its new owners the station would no longer suffer from the crippling debt it had carried for years.

'It's probably very frivolous of me,' she said, making up her mind with a rashness that had been foreign to her until she met Roman, 'but clothes are important.'

'If that is all,' he said coolly, 'buy some; I can afford them.'

In a voice spiked with ice, she returned, 'I'll buy them for myself, thank you.' Refusing to think of tomorrow, of any consequences, she looked at his beloved face. 'You said you have an appointment. I'll go shopping while you're doing that. What sort of party is this?'

His expression was unreadable. 'Old friends of mine are holding a pre-yearling sales party. Their guests will range from salt-of-the-earth horse people to sheikhs to Japanese industrial and financial moguls.'

In other words, totally out of her experience. Dismayed, she considered turning coward.

Sardonically Roman went on, 'My instinct is to tell you to cover up so that I don't have every man ogling you, but anything that emphasises those long legs and white skin would attract attention. If that's what you want.'

They looked at each other across the small table like old enemies. Smiling dangerously, Giselle met the challenge in his midnight eyes. 'Thanks for the help,' she said, and got to her feet.

He reached into a pocket and held out a card key. Brows raised, she looked at him silently. 'To my apartment at the hotel,' he said. 'Take the elevator to the top floor and this will let you in.'

Colour heated her cheeks. Fighting an odd reluctance, she took it from him.

They left the bar together; at the door, Roman looked down at her with gleaming eyes. 'Happy hunting. I should be back in three hours.'

Half an hour later, in an exclusive boutique, Giselle

stared at her reflection in shock. 'I can't go to an up-market party in this!'

The saleswoman, a chic middle-aged woman who remembered her from the days Leola had been the designer there, grinned. 'You look fabulous, and you know it.'

'It's not…partyish!'

'It's sexy as hell, and you told me you wanted sexy without being blatant, and no glitter. Which was a wise decision—you're not the glittery type. That sweater might be loose, but it's made of a blend of silk and merino, and every time you move—even when you breathe—it clings in all the right places. It's also long enough to act as a tiny miniskirt. The short sleeves and vee neck are sexy, even though the neckline doesn't show much cleavage.'

'Do you think so?' Giselle asked doubtfully. The neckline plunged just a little far for her comfort.

'I do. So will every man who looks at you.' She tweaked a long necklace so that it lay flat. 'And this pretty thing reinforces the fact that you've got lovely breasts.'

Too much, in Giselle's opinion. 'But tights,' she objected. 'They're casual wear.'

'On you they're rampant provocation,' the woman said airily. 'You've got fabulous legs. Opaque tights show them off without revealing any skin. The high courts are almost staid, but they make your legs look even longer, and the leather gloves are the final touch—completely sexy. Black suits you magnificently. Believe me, Giselle, you'll knock him—them—out!'

Giselle swallowed. 'I do look good,' she admitted, loving the voluptuous feel of the material across her shoulders. Beneath it she wore indecent underwear—a bra and tiny panties in black. 'But what if the others are dressed in sparkles?'

'Why should you care? Every woman there with half an ounce of fashion sense is going to ask you who your designer is. You'll be able to tell them it's your sister, and that they can buy these clothes from my boutique. In fact, if you do agree to wear it, I'll give you a decent discount.'

Giselle stared at her, then at herself in the mirror. Just this once she wanted to knock Roman's eyes out. And this outfit, outrageous as it was, would do it. She'd be blind not to see that it played up her strongest assets— her long legs and lithe figure, and the shoulders made muscular by hard work. As well, it revealed glimpses of the white skin that never tanned and that she found such a nuisance to care for—the skin Roman had told her he found so alluring.

Of course it cost megabucks, just about her share of what was left over from the sale of Parirua.

She swallowed. 'All right.'

'Do you know how to pull your hair back into a bun?'

'Yes.'

'Wear it on the back of your neck. And go easy on the make-up. However, you're one of the very few who can get away with a ruby lipstick. Leola would give her eye teeth to be able to wear this one.' She gave the name, then glanced at her watch. 'Look, why don't I give a friend of mine a call? She's a very clever make-up artist and I could see if she can make up your face some time this afternoon.'

In for a penny…Giselle nodded.

So just before five o'clock she found herself seated in front of a mirror that was cruelly reflective. And half an hour later she said in a wondering voice, 'That's amazing. I don't really look as though I've got anything on, just—better!'

The make-up artist nodded with satisfaction. 'You're not the obvious sort. Have fun!'

Giselle flushed. 'Thanks,' she said awkwardly, butter-flies invading her stomach—only somehow they'd transformed into a herd of buffalo.

So much so that she almost took the bus back to Maura's home. In the end it was the thought of one more night with Roman that clinched the matter. She'd bought these clothes for him, and she wasn't going to waste them, so she turned back from the bus stop, and headed purposefully for the hotel.

He was waiting when she walked into the suite, his jaw set. In a voice she'd never heard before he demanded, 'Where the hell have you been?'

'Buying things,' she said succinctly, her tone as curt as his.

He eyed the parcels in her arms, and his expression eased. 'So I see. Was it hard?'

'Yes,' she admitted, relaxing slightly. 'Did you have a lousy meeting?'

He opened the door into a room. 'Put them in here. And, no, the meeting was fine.'

'So why the frosty tone?'

He shrugged, his eyes meeting hers. 'I'm sorry for that. I thought you'd decided against coming. I don't like being stood up.'

He saw the colour wing up through her skin. Her eyes darkened, and Roman felt a surge of passion so intense it almost unmanned him.

'I thought about it,' she said gruffly as she walked into the dressing room, holding the parcels before her like a shield. 'I just hope you like the outfit. It's not at all conventional.'

'Neither are you.'

He wasn't going to tell her that he didn't care what she wore. His body tightened. Whatever she'd chosen wouldn't look as good as she'd look later, in his arms, when he'd stripped her of her clothes and they were together again in his bed.

They had dinner in the suite; Giselle realised he was careful not to touch her, and, although she longed for him, she accepted his restraint with a good grace.

But later, when she'd changed in the dressing room, she stood in front of the mirror and hoped with a fervour that made her feel slightly sick that he liked what he was about to see. She should have gone for spangles, she thought feverishly.

Well, it was too late now.

She turned and strode out into the sitting room, head high, shoulders very straight, her skin burning.

Magnificent in the stark black and white of evening clothes, he was standing by a table gazing down at something, and he swung around when he heard her come in. With heartbeats pounding in her ears and head held high, she stopped.

Not a muscle moved in his face. Lashes drooping, he examined her from head to toe, and then he smiled.

'That,' he purred in a voice that lifted the hair on the back of her neck, 'is a very clever outfit. Either you've been hiding the fact that you're a tease, or you let yourself be waylaid by a brilliant salesperson.'

'The second,' she blurted, so relieved that she could have wept.

'But you like yourself in it?'

'Yes,' she said boldly. 'Do you?'

He smiled again and came towards her with the slow, purposeful steps of a predator. 'I foresee a very tiring evening making sure every man in the room knows you came with me. Where did you find it?'

'I went to the boutique my sister used to design for until

she went overseas,' she confessed. 'They know me, and set me up with one of her designs.'

'And clearly she knows exactly how to bypass the trite and concentrate on seduction,' he said quietly. He held out something, something that glittered. 'Wear this.'

It was a bracelet—a fabulous thing in some silvery metal that might be platinum—set with stones that radiated crimson fire.

Numbly she shook her head.

'Why not?' he asked, jaw hardening.

'You didn't have to buy—' She bit back the words because she didn't know whether he was actually giving it to her or lending it.

Curtly he said, 'Then borrow it for the evening. Believe me, it will make everyone who looks at you take you very seriously indeed.'

How had he known that although she had dressed for him, she was still worried about how others would see the outfit? But she still didn't want to wear anything he'd bought her. And the bracelet seemed a lie, a prop. Jewellery like that belonged to mistresses...

Tension ached through her. She could refuse; she suspected that if she did he'd find some way to make sure she wore it. And anyway, what did it matter?

Surrendering, she held out her gloved hands. 'I don't think it would go with these.'

'Of course it will. Hold out your hand.'

She glanced up into eyes that were dark and commanding. A smile twisted her lips. 'You're going to have to do something about this habit you have of flinging orders around,' she said wryly, and held out her hand.

Frowning slightly, he eased the exquisite thing onto her wrist. 'I blame my upbringing,' he told her blandly.

At his touch, excitement beat, high and sharp, through her, heating her cheekbones, gleaming in her eyes.

She tried to hide it by saying, 'They're unusual stones—are they rubies?'

'Fire diamonds.'

'Oh.' Of course Giselle had heard of them, but she'd never expected to see one of the exotic gems found only on an Indian Ocean island. More precious than any other stones, they were so rare they were known as emperor gems, because only emperors had been able to afford them.

She looked down at the bracelet. 'It's very beautiful. I'll take great care of it.'

'But not, I think, as much care as I'll have to take of you.'

His words—and the distinctly territorial tone they were delivered in—lent her the confidence to cope with the next few hours. That, and the fact that Roman was never more than a pace away from her.

And it helped that their hosts, a striking couple called Nick and Perdita Dennison, were not only friends of Roman's, but that Giselle knew they were Northlanders like her. They owned a huge station in the central ranges.

Perdita Dennison had been a top model in her day; still exquisitely beautiful, she took one look at Giselle and exclaimed, 'You clever, clever girl! You look absolutely wonderful! You're one of the twins, aren't you—Maurice Foster's daughters?'

'Yes. My sister is the clothes designer.'

'If that outfit's any indication of her talent, she's a miracle—edgy and witty and just punk enough to be brilliant!' She leaned forward and gave Giselle a hug. 'Lovely to welcome another Northlander. There are a few more around here tonight, including our own twins. I'm so glad you could come.'

GET FREE BOOKS and a FREE MYSTERY GIFT WHEN YOU PLAY THE...

Just scratch off the silver box with a coin. Then check below to see the gifts you get!

SLOT MACHINE GAME!

YES! I have scratched off the silver box. Please send me the 4 FREE books and mystery gift for which I qualify. I understand I am under no obligation to purchase any books, as explained on the back of this card. I am over 18 years of age.

Mrs/Miss/Ms/Mr   Initials   **P8CI**

BLOCK CAPITALS PLEASE

Surname

Address

Postcode

7	7	7	**Worth FOUR FREE BOOKS plus a BONUS Mystery Gift!**
🍒	🍒	🍒	**Worth FOUR FREE BOOKS!**
♣	♣	♣	**Worth ONE FREE BOOK!**
🔔	🔔	🍒	**TRY AGAIN!**

Visit us online at www.millsandboon.co.uk

THE READER SERVICE™
FREE BOOK OFFER
FREEPOST CN81
CROYDON
CR9 3WZ

NO STAMP
NECESSARY
IF POSTED IN
THE U.K. OR N.I.

Her words gave Giselle the courage to view the glittering—in many cases literally—guests with equanimity. She hadn't met the Dennison twins, who were a couple of years younger than her, but Roman introduced her. A little to her surprise, she found herself enjoying their company, almost preening when they demanded to know where she'd bought her outfit. Roman was deep in conversation with a small, ancient Japanese man with a wise, humorous face, so she and the twins had a pleasant discussion about Leola's talent

Some hours later, after Roman had coolly and expeditiously sent off a South American polo player whose line of effusive compliments had rather embarrassed Giselle, she said, 'I knew our bloodstock industry was growing, but I didn't realise it was worldwide.'

'New Zealand breeds great horses,' he said. He sounded a little clipped, as though something had irritated him. 'Are you enjoying yourself?'

'Of course,' she said, pasting a smile onto her face. 'It's a wonderful occasion.'

'I didn't know you knew the Dennisons.'

'I hadn't met them, but I knew of them,' she said with a wry smile, her skin prickling between her shoulderblades. 'In New Zealand we don't have the usual six degrees of separation—at the most we have three, but usually it only takes two links to make a connection.'

His eyes kindled. 'And are you satisfied that spangles were definitely not the way to go?'

Before she could answer he lifted his head, a frown drawing his black brows together as he looked past her. It disappeared instantly, replaced by impassivity.

Giselle stiffened when a low, seductive voice said from behind her, 'Prince Roman, I'm so sorry to interrupt you, but I do need to thank you personally for the charming gift you sent me.'

A spasm of jealousy racked Giselle, shocking her with its primitive intensity. Lashes lowered, she watched as Roman nodded, his face a bronze mask.

'It was nothing,' he said negligently.

Bella Adams laughed and put a slim, pampered hand on his arm in a gesture that was both possessive and studied. Her ethereal beauty was displayed extravagantly in a slinky, champagne-coloured sheath that showed off her perfect body, and a diamond pendant that looked like something Marie Antoinette might have worn.

She was breathtaking, achieving an effortless glamour that shattered Giselle's cautious confidence into fragments.

'I love it,' she purred, and smiled up from beneath her lashes at Roman's expressionless face. 'I won't interrupt you any longer, but I had to tell you how much I value your thoughtfulness.'

Then, as if realising for the first time that there was someone with him, she turned and silently examined Giselle with a mocking little smile.

Her expression changed. Brows contracting into a frown, she said, 'Haven't we met?'

Giselle was almost certain the other woman hadn't seen her when she'd inadvertently spied on her with Roman on the beach. Very politely, she said, 'I don't think so.'

'Oh—well, no, I don't think we have, but for some weird reason you look vaguely familiar.' Dismissing Giselle, she bestowed a seductive smile on Roman. 'Thank you, sir.'

And glided away in a soft flurry of silk and delicious perfume.

Roman said casually, 'I'm sorry about that. Did you want me to introduce her? I can call her back if you do.'

Giselle wondered what he was sorry about—that he was with her when he could so obviously be with the lovely model, or that Bella Adams had been so rude?

Chin held high, she shrugged. 'It's all right,' she said stiltedly, wondering what small gift he'd given the star. And why he'd given it. For services rendered?

Another stab of jealousy stripped her of the last remnants of her confidence. Roman said something under his breath; she looked up and saw anger in his eyes, and a grim determination that chilled her.

Almost beneath his breath he ordered, 'Smile. The whole room is covertly eyeing us and our lovely hostess is wondering whether to come up and say something that will banish that frozen look from your face. I will not allow a foolish woman who means nothing to either of us to spoil your pleasure.'

Pride stiffened her spine. She met the unhidden command in his eyes with defiance, then grinned, a swift, challenging flash of white that brought an answering gleam to his eyes. He laughed deep in his throat, took her hand and lifted it to his lips.

The swift caress was enough, apparently. The chatter increased in volume.

Roman said thoughtfully, 'I think one of the things I enjoy so much about you is that I never know how you're going to react.'

After a startled glance Giselle tugged at her hand, but he kept it in his, his fingers folding warmly around hers.

'Kissing hands is so old-fashioned that no one does it now,' he remarked, holding her a little too close to his side. 'And even when it was popular the salutation was usually delivered to a dowager rather than her debutante granddaughter.'

'It certainly defused my temper,' she lied brightly. Not only was she still furious with Bella Adams, but her heart was cold and forlorn. Yet she had no right to ask him what his relationship with the woman was—or had been.

Giselle intended to stick to her side of their bargain, but, oh, she wished the model hadn't appeared out of nowhere tonight. Until then she'd let herself relax in Roman's company—well, almost. The passionate craving that had been building deep inside her prevented anything but a superficial ease.

But the charade had exploded in her face, and all she wanted to do was crawl into a hole and hide. Although Roman wasn't going to let her do that, and, anyway, pride dictated that she follow his lead. She'd probably never see anyone from this throng again, and apart from anything else she didn't want to spoil Perdita Dennison's party.

So she fixed a smile to her face, wondering just how Bella Adams had been invited.

One of the Dennison twins enlightened her a little later. 'She's an old friend of Mum's,' she said cheerfully. 'Well, not exactly a friend; Mum helped her get her first job, apparently. When she heard Bella was going to be in Auckland she invited her; apparently her marriage is under pressure, and she's feeling miserable.' She pulled a face. 'That's no excuse for bad manners, though.'

No indeed, Giselle thought vengefully, watching the other woman make a scintillating progress around the room.

CHAPTER SEVEN

An hour later Roman said levelly, 'Time to go.'

Giselle met his eyes, and her breath locked in her throat at his intent, focused gaze. His unspoken hunger beat against her, a potent, tangible force that summoned a matching response from her. She said, 'Yes.'

'Back to my suite.'

The words hung in the air like a challenge.

Giselle nodded. 'Yes,' she said again, burning every last bridge with a fierce joy.

They searched out their hosts. Trying hard to keep her mind off what was going to happen when they reached the hotel, Giselle noted the way Nick Dennison looked at his wife. He wasn't a man who gave away much—like Roman, he kept his expressions under control—but when he smiled at Perdita Giselle saw love in his eyes, deep and all-encompassing, and she envied the older woman with a strength that shocked her.

That was what she hungered for—and what she'd never get. Oh, Roman wanted her for now, but she didn't belong in his world. He'd marry some suitable woman—a princess or aristocrat's daughter, perhaps; certainly someone who'd have all the attributes a man like Roman needed in a wife.

But she had tonight, she reminded herself staunchly.

And after that she'd make an end to it; she didn't have the stamina to be a part-time mistress, available on the rare occasions he came to New Zealand. Not when she loved him with all her heart.

Perdita Dennison smiled at her. 'Both my daughters admire your panache,' she said, and added, 'Now that we've met, we mustn't lose touch. I'm so glad you came tonight.'

She turned to Roman, who'd just finished shaking hands with her husband. 'Lovely to see you again, Roman—next time you must stay longer. Give my love to Jacoba, won't you, when you meet her next.'

Giselle blinked, then realised that Jacoba was Princess Jacoba, who'd been a supermodel and was now married to Prince Marco, a cousin of the ruling prince of Illyria. Roman had said something about his two cousins marrying New Zealanders, but Jacoba had been born Illyrian. However, she'd grown up in Northland, and clearly she knew the Dennisons.

'I'll do that,' he promised.

Outside he said, 'Did you like them?'

'Very much,' she returned.

Once in the hotel Roman locked the door and turned to her, eyes narrowed and intense, his face harshly drawn. 'Now,' he said between his teeth, '*now* I can do what that outfit's been taunting every man with all evening—discover what's beneath it. Slowly...'

And he drew her close and kissed her, his previous gentleness abandoned in a storm of headstrong passion.

Giselle went up like a torch, yielding to the desire that had been building ever since she'd seen him again. Nothing, she thought dazedly as his mouth plundered hers, was going to stand in the way of the white-hot consummation she needed so much.

After all, the memory was going to have to last a lifetime...

Eventually he lifted her and carried her through the suite, his mouth still on hers. She clung, avid for the pleasure his kiss brought, relishing the shift and flow of the coiled muscles against her, knowing that for these precious moments his power and his strength were hers to command.

When he slid her to her feet she realised they were in his bedroom. The bed had already been pulled back, the lamps turned low.

Trembling inside, she began to strip off her glove, but he said, 'No.'

She looked at him in bewilderment. 'What?'

'Take off the necklace, not the glove.'

Little chills ran down her spine. Did he want some sort of striptease—and did she have the nerve to do it? Yes, she thought, yes, I can, but it's going to be reciprocal!

'You take off your tie first.' Her voice sounded odd—mocking, a little husky, wholly seductive. Almost, she thought incredulously, as though she knew what she was doing!

With a taut smile he undid the black tie and dropped it on the floor. She lifted the beads over her head and aimed them to land on top of the tie. 'Now what?' she asked.

He said, 'The sweater.' His lips barely moved and she could see a pulse throbbing in his jaw, but he was undoing the studs on his dress shirt.

Reckless abandon fountained through her. Raising the hem, she shimmied the garment over her head, holding it for a second in one hand while she stood revealed in her scandalous black bra and the tights and gloves. On her wrist the fire diamonds burned in a dazzle, echoing the passion that scorched through her skin, bringing with it sensation and longing and a desperate desire that ate into her composure.

Watching him, she saw the effort it took for him to keep his expression under rigid control, and waited three heart-beats before she let the sweater go. He couldn't hide the darkness of his gaze, or that betraying jerk of some tiny muscle against his hard jaw.

Inwardly exulting, her body swept by surges of heat along every nerve, she bargained, 'You next—your shirt.'

It came off in one powerful swish, and she felt her heart burst within her. He was so—so utterly male, so tall and bronzed and lean, that she thought she might just die of desire.

She said unevenly, 'You are beautiful.'

His eyes burned. In a low, dangerous tone he said, 'From you that means something, but you encompass all the beauty in this room. All night you've been tantalising me with glimpses of that white skin and the knowledge that soon I'd be able to see you, take out the pins that imprison your glorious hair and make you mine again.'

She took a step towards him, but he held up his hands. 'Finish what you started,' he said harshly. 'I don't dare touch you.'

After she kicked off her shoes she unashamedly watched while he stepped out of his shoes and socks and stripped down his trousers.

Her breath locked in her throat at his sleek magnificence.

Roman's long fingers were clenched into fists at his sides. Dark and powerful, his handsome face set, he watched her carefully, slowly, ease off the gloves, then sit down on the bed and unroll the tights and let them fall in a small heap.

Heart pounding, she began to stand, but her knees refused to work. She looked down at the fire diamonds on her bare arm. 'I don't…' Her voice seized up. She swallowed and started again, 'I don't think I can…'

He laughed low in his throat and came across, kneeling in front of her. 'Good,' he said, and pushed her down onto the bed.

Somehow he managed to remove the remaining scandalous scraps of lace and silk as he came down beside her, and bent his head to kiss the soft mound of one breast, then the other. Closing her eyes, Giselle shocked herself with an urgent groan, and linked her hands around his waist, pulling him against her, desperate for the fulfilment only he could give her.

Just this once…

The words hammered in her ears. This would be the last time they'd spend together, so she'd make the most of it. She opened her eyes and shuddered as his lips found the aching tip of her breast. Heat spiralled through her, fire and energy impossibly mingling in a lassitude that melted her bones. Languidly she lifted her hand and brushed the black hair back from his brow, revelling in its crisp caress against her fingers.

The glint of the fire diamonds made her stiffen. Instantly he lifted his head. 'What is it?' he asked gutturally.

'I should take off the bracelet,' she managed.

He gave a slow, wolfish smile. 'Leave it,' he commanded.

And he bent his head again, his mouth closing around her breast. An aching moan caught in her throat. She arched in involuntary supplication, her desire almost peaking. He moved his hand down, down, down, and at the first touch of his fingers she went rigid, then convulsed beneath their gentle, skilful manipulation.

Before she'd descended from the first erotic release he had moved into her, sending her all the way back up that reckless staircase. Waves of sensation began to build as her body adjusted to his weight and the subtle intrusion of his presence. She caught the rhythm and began to move with him, their bodies locked, their hearts blending. Gradually, intently, each new sensation intensifying the clamour of reckless desire, he pushed her further and further towards another orgasm, using his body as an instrument of pleasure until she choked out his name and unravelled in his arms.

He thrust again and again, and together they found the height of fulfilment, rocketing into a place where only ecstasy existed.

Later, still locked against him, Giselle breathed in the scent of their love-making, clinging to the rapture that was ebbing inexorably away as she tried to imprint every sensory impression so she'd never forget.

He kissed her, and her arms tightened around him. He said something in what she supposed was Illyrian, then laughed huskily. 'Let me go, my lovely one. I'll crush you.'

'No,' she said.

But he turned effortlessly onto his back, pulling her with him. A massive yawn shook her, and she ached with sorrow, because she didn't want to sleep.

'Stay there,' he ordered, and lethargic with exhaustion and satiation she slid into a sleep more refreshing than she'd ever known before.

Giselle woke to a kiss, and the sinfully arousing caress of a hand over her breast. 'Is it morning?' she said sleepily after she'd returned the kiss with interest.

'It's nine-thirty,' Roman told her, amusement colouring his voice. 'And I am due at a meeting in twenty minutes, so I have to leave you, my beautiful girl. Go back to sleep.'

But she watched him leave through lowered lashes, and

into her heart there crept hope. They had made love several more times; he'd been insatiable—as, she admitted without any remorse, had she.

And the last time had been so shattering that afterwards she'd wept in his arms; passion she could cope with, but this time Roman's love-making totally undermined her.

Perhaps there was chance for them after all? Surely he couldn't make love like that—with such tender rapacity—if he didn't feel something for her?

Get real, she told herself stringently. Of course he felt something for her. He enjoyed her company. He might even like her. Certainly, he wanted her.

None of that meant he was in love with her.

Yet she lay quietly in the big bed, listening to the sounds of an Auckland morning, and her heart refused to accept that there wasn't a chance for them. Her decision to make this their last night together seemed cowardly. Surely she had enough courage to fight for what she wanted?

Running away never solved anything.

So she wouldn't run. She'd stick it out.

Filled with boundless energy, she bounced out of bed and showered, leaving her face free of make-up. Then she picked up the clothes she'd discarded last night—now neatly stacked onto a chair, she noted—and hung them in the wardrobe. She'd gone to sleep wearing the bracelet; she looked at it for a long moment, then reluctantly took it off and slid it into the drawer of the bedside table.

Suddenly ravenous, she looked around for the hotel folder, found the menu in it and ordered breakfast from room service.

The knock came sooner than she'd expected; smiling, she went across to let in the waiter—a smile that rapidly faded when she saw Bella Adams standing there.

'I've remembered where I saw you,' the model said abruptly, scrutinising her with sharp, assessing eyes. 'I've got a very good memory for faces. In Paris, at the party after Chanel's showing. You were blonde then—that tawny-gold colour that's so hard to get just right. You were with Roman, and it was totally obvious that you were head over heels in love with him.'

Indignantly, Giselle opened her mouth to refute the accusation—then realised who she was talking about. *Leola.*

Leola had been with Roman. Her mind flew to the photograph in the magazine—the one she'd dumped in Fala'isi. It had been Leola after all...

Nausea gripped her. She'd known all along, she thought wearily; she'd refused to accept it because she'd fallen in love with him straight away.

She felt the colour drain from her skin, and had to concentrate on standing upright. Oh—my poor Leola! she thought, hating Roman Magnati with a passion.

Bella Adams smiled triumphantly. 'Well, sweetie, enjoy him while you've got him, but don't make any plans.' She ran a scornful glance down Giselle's plain white T-shirt and very ordinary jeans. 'God knows what he sees in you, but he's going to want to stop slumming soon, and when he does you'll be out the door so fast you won't know what's hit you. Mind you, he's known for his very nice parting gifts.'

'Like the one he gave you?' Giselle said, fighting for control.

The other woman said contemptuously, 'Men don't value what they can have for free. That was a promise, not a parting gift.'

And she walked away, hips swaying, shoulders erect, while Giselle shut the door and stumbled across the room to find a chair.

She dragged in several great, gulping breaths, then shuddered. Had he and Leola been lovers?

'Oh, God, *no*,' she whispered, shaking with disgust. Surely not?

But she remembered things—the alteration in Leola's voice when she'd spoken of him, her evasiveness, Giselle's conviction that something had gone wrong in her sister's life. Tiny, intangible clues…

Individually they meant nothing. Together with the photograph—well, it was circumstantial evidence, but with Bella Adams' recognition they added up to something that turned her stomach.

The model had been telling the truth; she didn't know they were twins, and she had been utterly sure it was Giselle she'd seen in Paris. Giselle felt as though she were covered in slime, her hopes of a few minutes ago crumbling into dust.

Was Roman acting out some sick fantasy, bedding twin sisters? Was he even now comparing their performance? It would explain so much—his unexpected interest in her, his passion…even, she thought, her throat closing, his tenderness.

Why hadn't Leola told her? Because she was ashamed? Because it was over? No, Giselle thought with bleak pragmatism; probably because she realised there'd be no future in any relationship with a prince.

Except that Leola would fit in anywhere, she thought fiercely as she got to her feet.

Obsessing over what had gone wrong with Leola's life wasn't going to get her out of here before Roman came back. She should stay and face him, but her courage only stretched so far, and she couldn't bear the thought of such a confrontation. Learning one day that she loved him, and the next that he'd betrayed her, had shattered her.

No, it wasn't love. She could never love a man she didn't respect, and she couldn't respect a man who'd deliberately played with hearts.

So this aching, savage pain wasn't caused by love; it was simply carnal passion, a heated, degrading desire she'd learn to overcome.

Hurrying into the bedroom, she began to stack her clothes into their shopping bags while keeping her gaze averted from the tumbled bed. Her first instinct—to run as far and as fast as she could, to hide in some bolt-hole like a wounded animal, had to be dismissed. Her bolt-hole was Parirua, and yesterday she'd signed a contract to stay there for six months.

Yet if she went back home, it wouldn't be hard for him to find her. He knew roughly where she lived. All he had to do was ask the Dennisons.

Well, if he did, she thought staunchly, by then she'd have regained enough backbone and she'd tell him exactly what she thought of him!

Desperately she packed, then wrote a note in case he felt obliged to come looking for her. The agony was too raw for her to cope with, so she made it plain and simple.

Thank you for last night and goodbye. I think it best that we don't see each other again.

It smacked of hypocrisy when she wanted to slap him senseless, to make him realise how humiliated she felt, how much she hated him for what he'd done to both her and Leola. Somehow the birth of that tentative hope only a few minutes ago had made things so much worse.

Stony-faced, she caught the bus to Maura's town house on the North Shore. Yet an hour later, when she was driving her old car along the highway north, she was tense, waiting for—what?

Roman wouldn't follow. Why would he? Whatever degrading fantasy he'd been playing out with twin sisters had been fulfilled; surely he'd realise that once they knew neither she nor Leola would have anything to do with him now.

Because of course she'd have to tell her sister.

Bile rose, and she gagged, but she kept driving steadily north, intent on reaching Parirua. Once she was there she'd be all right, she thought desperately. It—and Leola—were was the only constants in her life; they had never failed her.

Giselle pushed back a strand of wet black hair and glowered down at the mud. 'This is supposed to be summer,' she told her horse wearily.

The gelding didn't react. Like her, it was aiming to reach home with the least amount of effort and time. Squaring her shoulders, Giselle looked around with tired eyes, checking the damage the storm had wrought. The rain had washed away parts of the track, and the rest of it needed resurfacing.

'Presumably the new owners will get into that,' she said aloud, flicking the reins against the horse's neck. And the rain had been sorely needed; this downpour, warm and dense from the Tropics, had come to Parirua just in time to offer a thin chance for the place to break even this year.

Not that that meant anything to her now.

Before she'd spent those impassioned nights in Roman's arms the sale of Parirua had seemed the ultimate betrayal. But the real betrayal had been the magazine covers she'd seen since; photographs of Roman with Bella Adams, and the headlines that screamed PRINCE TO MARRY MODEL?

Apparently the woman was now Roman's constant

escort. And, judging by the looks they were exchanging, both he and she were very happy together.

Occasionally Giselle wondered if Bella Adams had lied to her. She wouldn't have put it past her, but not even that frail hope stood up to the light of day. The woman had been utterly convinced she'd seen Giselle with Roman in Paris.

And the worst of it was that, for the first time in their lives, Giselle couldn't bring herself to confide in her sister. Her cowardice made her feel sick, but if Leola had had an affair with Roman she'd be humiliated to discover that he'd also seduced Giselle.

And presumably Leola knew about his new romance; she was certainly hurting. That familiar connection between them meant that they were feeling each other's pain. At least, Giselle thought wearily, urging her mount down a muddy slope, Leola would be putting her twin's misery down to losing Parirua.

It had been hard to tell her that after the mortgage had been settled and the tax debt paid there'd be a bare few thousand dollars left for her.

'Oh, hell,' Leola said in a defeated tone. She sounded tired.

Giselle bit her lip. 'Are you all right?' she asked carefully.

There was a pause. 'I'm OK,' Leola told her, her voice dragging a little. 'I've just—well, I've just finished a relationship, and I'm feeling a bit down. But you know me—I'll soon be fine.'

Giselle's heart ached, but her sister's words had been confirmation of everything she feared. 'I'm sorry. Are you planning to come back? If you are, you can have my share if it would be useful.' Other New Zealand designers had achieved success starting locally and exporting, and Leola had the drive and the talent to succeed.

'You're a darling,' her sister said after a moment, 'but

I'm learning too much to come home yet. What are you going to do when the six months is up?'

'I'll think of something,' Giselle told her sturdily, wishing she could help her sister somehow, furious with Roman Magnati for the havoc he'd wrought.

Somehow she'd find a job, either on a farm or in some agriculturally related business. She had skills; she could put them to use.

She chirruped to the gelding as the rain came down again. By the time she reached the homestead, old and once gracious beside the sea, she was drenched, every muscle in her body ached, and she wanted nothing more than a bath. First of all, however, she had to deal with the horse and feed the two cattle dogs.

Once inside she discovered that the power was off, not unusual during a storm. Muttering, she lit the ancient range in the kitchen.

She could cook dinner on it. Except that she didn't want any. She seemed to have lost her appetite over the past month and had to force herself to eat.

While she waited for the water to heat she stripped off her muddy clothes and got into a robe, then checked the mail.

Nothing.

Of course there was nothing. It was stupid and pathetic to look for something from Roman; he wasn't going to think of her again, let alone contact her. Their conversation the night she'd arrived back in Parirua had conclusively put an end to their brief affair, and made sure he'd never contact her again.

Giselle's hand had shaken as she'd lifted the receiver and said, 'Hello.'

'Why?' he demanded.

She'd already known what she was going to say; during

the long drive home she'd planned it. 'Because this is real life,' she said steadily, her voice cool and remote. 'It was terrific, but if we hadn't met in Auckland yesterday it wouldn't have happened again. I don't want to be an accidental, part-time lover. Goodbye, Roman. It's been great, but it's over.'

CHAPTER EIGHT

'I SEE.' Roman's voice was very formal. 'Thank you for being so frank. I wish you happiness, and every success. By the way, you left something behind. I'll courier it up to you.'

And he hung up.

Giselle had sagged into a chair, then curled over and hugged herself as tears stung behind her eyes. It had taken every bit of strength she possessed, but she'd sent him away and now she'd never see him again.

'So you can put it down to experience and get on with life,' she told herself sturdily. 'You don't love him, and passion dies when it's starved. In a year's time you'll be fine.'

Getting on with her life proved to be more difficult than she'd imagined. First of all, the 'something' she'd left behind turned out to be the fire diamond bracelet. Insulted and hurt, she'd tried to contact Roman, but the hotel refused to pass on his address.

She'd thought of asking the Dennisons, but her experience with the hotel had made her wary, and she didn't want Perdita Dennison to think of her as a sleazy hanger-on. The cynical gesture of using it to pay her off sickened her; beautiful as the bracelet was, she couldn't bear to look at it. She got nowhere when she tried researching his address on the internet, beyond finding out that he seemed to have residences in London, New York and Illyria.

After fruitlessly turning over ways to get the hateful bracelet safely to him without paying huge insurance costs, she'd put it in the safe to deal with later.

Since then she'd spent several weeks of aching emptiness. She'd been so naïve, convinced she could deal with the aftermath of their time together; what she hadn't truly understood was that his love-making had altered her in the most fundamental way. She longed for him, a sharp, intense yearning that stripped her world of colour and meaning and took all the savour from it.

Now—too late—she understood why her father had spent his life grieving for the wife who'd left him—and why her mother had committed suicide rather than face an existence without her lover.

Not that she'd do that, but she'd never been so utterly, shatteringly lonely.

At least she had work to occupy her. Each day she spent out on the station, trying to submerge her thoughts in hard physical labour, and at night, when the evenings stretched before her, she kept telling herself that this bitter grief couldn't last for ever. Roman simply wasn't worth it.

Besides, the new owners had asked for a list of immediate concerns, and she was busy formulating that and finding out approximate costs.

She stacked a few papers neatly on the old desk, and stood listening to the rain on the corrugated iron roof. It was easing off, signalling the passing of the storm.

'I'll manage,' she said eventually.

She had to.

At least she wasn't pregnant. Efficient in everything he did, Roman had made sure of that. So why did she spend a lot of time wishing that, just once, their protection had failed?

Because she was an idiot. He wasn't even an honourable man, and he'd caused a gap between her and Leola that might never heal. The thought of being treated like actors in a porn film infuriated her.

Grim-faced, she walked across to the window. The rain stopped as though someone had turned off a tap, and as she watched the clouds began to lift, a cleft in them revealing the thin hook of moon in the western sky. At the end of the garden the narrow harbour shimmered across to the hills on the other side.

Tiger country, her grandfather used to call those hills, eyeing the steep, dark cliffs and gullies that were heavily covered in Northland's untamed, luxuriant rainforest.

'They're no good for anything,' he'd say, 'except to shield us from the cold southerlies.'

But Giselle loved them, proudly defiant against the horizon.

A distant noise brought a swift frown. Thunder? No, it sounded like an engine. She held her breath as her ears strained to distinguish the sound.

'A chopper!' she said starkly, and whirled.

Not only was it a helicopter, but it was sinking lower and lower.

And in the aftermath of a storm, with night thickening every second, that had to mean an emergency.

By the time it landed on the beach below the house Giselle had scrambled into the first clothes to hand, a pair of skimpy shorts and a very old, saggy T-shirt. Devoutly hoping the shirt was loose enough to hide the fact that she hadn't bothered with a bra, she slid her feet into boots and went out of the house, letting off one of the dogs on her way down to the beach.

Once there, she and the dog stopped beneath one of the huge pohutukawa trees that lined the sand. The pitch of the chopper's engines altered; the rotors slowed, and the pilot began to shut down.

She waited tensely, her eyes rapidly accustoming themselves to the darkness so that when the door of the chopper slid back and a man leapt lithely to the ground, she could see him quite clearly in the wan light of the moon.

Tall—well over six feet—and magnificently built, Giselle realised with an odd twist in her stomach as he came towards her.

A sinuous little chill snaked down her spine. The unconscious set of his broad shoulders breathed an arrogant acknowledgement that set her teeth on edge, and he walked on the wet sand with a silent, deliberate grace that was all predatory male.

Someone of extremely forceful presence—enough to intimidate at fifty paces—and, judging by his mode of transport, he also had stacks of money.

Roman.

Fierce pride stiffened her shoulders and her spine. However much she despised him, her exposure to his powerful brand of charisma had taught her that she was alarmingly vulnerable to him.

What the *hell* was he doing here?

Roman stopped. 'I can see you, Giselle.'

She'd been hoping for—what? She didn't know. His voice—level, with that faint, fascinating trace of an accent—showed absolutely no emotion.

A little flame of electricity, enough to bring dismay in its wake, mingled with the pain of betrayal. Hot anger took her by surprise; she could feel it charging every cell in her body. *Dignity*, she reminded herself fiercely; it's not much, but it's all you've got left.

Walking out into the thin moonlight, she stopped and asked, 'What are you doing here?'

He paused before saying, 'I came to see how you are.'

'I'm fine,' she told him with icy precision.

'We need to talk.'

Giselle didn't move. 'Do we? I thought I'd said everything there was to say.'

'We said nothing—you made sure of that by running away. First of all, are you pregnant?'

'No,' she said, obscurely comforted that he'd taken the trouble to come and find out. At least he had some honour. Had he done the same for Leola?

Nausea warred with a feverish hunger. Through her lashes she scanned the darkly arrogant angles of his face, shuttered against her to reveal nothing of the transient passion that belonged to their previous meetings.

He seemed completely relaxed, impervious self-assurance radiating from him like an aura when he said, 'Invite me in.'

She didn't move. 'Why?'

'Because a few weeks ago I bought this property.'

Giselle's heart literally stopped in her chest. Stunned, she blinked and met eyes as cold and forbidding as the deepest reaches of the sea.

It took every ounce of fortitude she possessed to say stonily, 'Parirua was sold to MegaCorp.'

'MegaCorp?'

Oh, how could she have been so stupid? That idiotic name, coined in a moment of sarcastic playfulness, had come back to haunt her. He must think she was mad. Or a halfwit.

Stumbling over the words, she muttered, 'It's a joke—some firm that has Holdings in its name.'

'Byzantium Holdings—which belongs to me.' His voice was as frigid as his gaze.

An outraged fury blocked any coherent thoughts, until with a superhuman effort she reasserted control. 'So was that the reason for the big seduction?' Before he could answer she added contemptuously, 'You didn't need to go to those lengths to make sure of the sale.'

He didn't like that. His chin came up in a single, uncompromising movement and his eyes narrowed. A dark figure in the moonlight, he looked truly formidable. Her treacherous heart ached with loss and chagrin and a fierce untamed longing.

In a crisp, forbidding voice he asked, 'Would knowing I owned Byzantium have made the decision to sell easier for you?'

'There was no decision to be made—I *had* to sell. Tell me one thing. Did you know I owned Parirua when you—when we met on the island?'

Mouth tightening, Roman Magnati said a single abrupt word in some liquid language. 'When we met, no.'

'But you soon found out,' she stated, knowing it was true, knowing when he had.

'The day before I left. Which was why I went. I don't mix business with pleasure. Ever.'

'So what was Auckland all about, then? You'd come to sign the property deeds, I suppose.'

'I didn't need to be there for that,' he said abruptly. 'I came because I thought you might be upset at losing the station.'

Could she believe him? No, she thought, clamping down on an urgent plea from some treacherous part of her to

accept his words. 'Why didn't you tell me then—in
Auckland—that it was you who'd bought Parirua?'

He shrugged. 'I tried. If you remember, you stopped me
in very blunt terms. And I let it lie, because I thought I had
plenty of time to tell you. If you'd stayed, you'd have
known before lunchtime.'

Driven by anguish and a cold, still anger, she said
bleakly, 'After you'd softened me up by a night of wild
passion? Well, you can find another manager. I'll leave as
soon as I get the house cleared out.'

There was a moment's silence before he said silkily,
'I'm afraid that your pique—while understandable—in
no way negates the contract. If you pull out there will be
penalties.'

Bracing herself, she ignored the icy pooling of fear
beneath her ribs. 'What sort of penalties?'

'If you go, your workers go also.'

The foreboding solidified into shock. 'But—they can't
do that. They have nowhere to go, and, anyway, this is not
their fight! They've done nothing to deserve that treatment.'

'I am the owner; I have the right to make use of my
property as I think fit,' he said with an intimidating ruthlessness.

'They have no jobs to go to, no income,' she protested,
searching a face that was iron-hard and closed against her.
A chilling fear wore down her defiance.

He shrugged. 'Why should I care?''

'I can go,' she said, white-faced and searching for a com-
promise. 'But you'll need someone to work the station. Joe
and Rangi are good at their jobs. They know Parirua intimately; in fact, Joe managed it for me while I was on holiday.'

His eyes narrowed and his voice dropped a further few
tones. 'As far as I am concerned, Giselle, you and the

workers come as a package,' he said softly. 'If you stay, they stay. If you go, they go.'

'Why?' she asked woodenly, adding on a spurt of anger, 'You can't possibly want me to stay. I thought I'd made it obvious that any further relationship with you is out of the question.'

'You did.' His tone was laced with contempt. 'I have no need of or desire for an unwilling mistress. But I plan to develop Parirua, and having someone who knows everyone in the area will help that process.'

Giselle seized on the one word that registered. '*Develop* Parirua? Plonk houses all over it? Clutter every bay with mock-Mediterranean mansions? Destroy the natural beauty of the place and turn it into a fake suburb with swimming pools in every backyard?' Anger sizzled through every word—anger and a vast disillusionment that led her to finish hotly, 'How dare you organise such—such *sacrilege*? If you think I'd be a willing part of that you're utterly mistaken.'

His eyes narrowed again, and a primal chill iced her skin. 'Do we have to stand on the beach discussing this?'

The dog at her feet relaxed, and some of her tension dissipated at the sounds of Joe's arrival. A short, nuggety, dearly familiar figure, he ranged up beside her, asking, 'Everything OK, Giselle?'

'Are you Joe Watene?' Roman asked abruptly.

Joe said, 'Yes.'

'I am Roman Magnati, the new owner of Parirua.'

Joe thrust out his hand. 'Pleased to meet you,' he said.

Giselle glanced up at Roman. He looked like some antique statue, beautiful yet iron-hard, and then he moved slightly and she saw a predator, all lean, sleek aggression and power.

And in spite of everything that had happened—his

betrayal, her disillusion—she still wanted him. After the dull misery of the past weeks she was alive again, her brain in full gear, her body alert and responsive, every cell charged with energy.

Sexual craving, she thought scornfully. That was all it was.

OK, so she was more like her parents than she'd thought, but *she* wasn't going to surrender to it and spend the rest of her life longing for a man she despised. He might be superb in bed, she thought bleakly, hating the fierce clutch of response in the pit of her stomach at that thought, and he still invaded her dreams so that she woke most mornings after a night caught in the snare of feverish memories, but she had to be strong enough to chisel him out of her heart and her life.

When the two men had gone through the ritual of hand-shaking, she said woodenly, 'You'd better come up to the house. With any luck the power will be on again.'

'Wasn't when I left home,' Joe informed her in a gloomy voice.

They walked back through the garden, overgrown but heavy with the perfume of gardenias and the huge datura tree, its white trumpets gleaming in the rapidly fading light.

Inside, the house was dark, smelling of age and three days of constant rain. Giselle led them into the kitchen, warm enough by then to bring a bead of sweat to her brow. She tried to light the ancient hurricane lamp, muttering silently to herself as the wretched thing refused to co-operate. It was a small thing, but she gave a noiseless sigh when at last the flame glimmered and steadied as she adjusted the mantle to throw out a warm pool of light.

Something feral and hot burned into life inside Giselle when she saw Roman's face clearly again.

He was impossibly handsome, but it was his eyes that

caught and held her—so dark they were unreadable, with glinting, glittering gold flecks like stars in a night sky. Compelling, magnetic, they seemed to see right through her.

A dark magician, she thought. A *treacherous* dark magician...

'I'd better go,' Joe said, looking from one to the other. His eyes lingered on Roman's angular face, and he gave a little nod, as though trusting what he saw there.

Joe, Giselle realised with a twist of pain, accepted the prince at face value.

In a smooth, faintly derisory voice, Roman said, 'Perhaps Ms Foster would prefer you to stay.'

Giselle made up her mind. 'It's OK, Joe. Prince Roman and I have quite a bit to discuss.'

As Joe left she turned away from the man watching her and asked coldly, 'What would you like to drink? I have tea and coffee, or some of my father's whisky.'

'If you can make coffee, I'd like that, thank you.'

'I can make that,' she said with a touch of acid. 'We have a stove percolator. Sit down at the table, and I'll get some for you.'

But he remained standing and looked around the large, old-fashioned kitchen, his brows drawing together as he noted its sore need of paint and refurbishment. 'I am sorry to have literally dropped in on you at such an inopportune time.'

Reacting to the note of mockery in his impersonal tone, she returned crisply, 'It would have been nice to have been forewarned.'

'If I had, would you have been here?'

She shrugged. 'Why not?'

It wasn't exactly a lie. Where else would she go?

'Indeed, why not?' His voice was smooth and indolent, revealing nothing.

No doubt he was pleased she was showing such calmness. Men, she had heard, hated it when discarded lovers made a fuss.

Of course, she'd been the one to discard him...

Salvaging what pride she could from that thought, she filled the kettle from the filter jug. 'I didn't realise you could fly a chopper.'

But then, she knew so little about him.

His broad shoulders lifted. 'It never came up, did it?' Before she could react to the ironic note in his voice, he went on, 'Does the power go off every time there is a storm?'

Welcome to the backblocks, she thought, fighting back a surge of bitterness. Aloud she told him, 'Usually. Parirua is at the end of the line, and in a high wind branches come down and break the cable. Sometimes the road slips and carries away a pole.'

'So why doesn't your supplier restore the power?'

'Because Parirua isn't the only property affected. The linesmen will get here eventually.' She reached up into the dresser and collected two mugs. 'Further down the road the dairy farmers need electricity to milk night and morning—naturally, they get priority.'

'I see.' He glanced at a thin gold watch on his wrist.

'It will probably be on by tomorrow morning.'

Keep your voice even, she reminded herself, reaching for the coffee container.

However she made the mistake of looking sideways to catch him surveying her with a hooded, dangerous look. He held her gaze for a feverish second, and a slow, infinitely ambiguous smile barely lifted the sculpted lines of his mouth.

Acutely aware of the fact that she wore no bra, she ignored the heat burning her skin and wrenched off the lid.

Her tongue felt thick in her dry mouth and every cell in

her body vibrated with awareness, but she managed to say evenly, 'It's surprising how easy it is to run this house without power; it was built before the days of electricity, so it's just a matter of slipping back in time. What I really find difficult is that the telephone line is so overburdened I often can't get onto the internet. And of course we have no cell phone coverage.'

And perhaps that will make you reconsider this development plan, she thought furiously, spooning coffee into the plunger. The silence was broken only by the quiet hissing of the kettle before it broke into song.

Giselle had turned to make the coffee when Roman said, 'That is certainly an inconvenience.'

Maliciously cheered by the effect of her words, she opened the tin that held the shortbread and set a tray with the usual milk and sugar, then carried it across to the table.

'Are you joining me?' he asked.

'Of course.' Although tension was screwing her nerves to a painful pitch, she sat down.

Roman lowered himself into the chair opposite, leaning back to watch her pour the coffee. She felt the faint tremor of her hands, and concentrated on pouring cleanly and quickly. For some reason he was deliberately, wordlessly reminding her that they had been lovers, that although she might have sent him away she was still ferociously attracted to him.

He might know women, she thought with desperate courage, but he didn't understand her. No matter how much discipline it took, she'd never give in to this humiliating passion again. 'Your coffee,' she said.

He reached out a hand, but after a taut second she set the cup and saucer down on the table in front of him. No way was she going to risk touching him. Furious though she was with him, she didn't dare.

A taunting little smile touched his lips. He said nothing, however, until after the first sip. 'This is excellent. Where do you get it?'

'The family up the road keep me supplied,' she told him, furious with herself for being pleased at his surprise. 'They source their beans worldwide, and have worked out blends to suit the locals. They're doing very well selling to various restaurants and coffee bars around the north. When they came here for lunch one day they nobly forced down the coffee I gave them before offering to supply us too.'

'This is an excellent biscuit too,' he told her blandly. 'Did you make it?'

'Yes. It's my grandmother's recipe.'

He nodded as though she'd confirmed something. He'd probably been astonished at the contrast between her and her sister—Giselle with their mother's colouring and her hayseed naivety, Leola with her cosmopolitan sophistication. It took a sharp eye to notice that feature by feature they were almost identical.

Nausea gripped her. She gulped down some coffee and wondered wildly how she was going to stop herself from throwing it at his lying, handsome face.

And then the lights flickered on and off, then on, settling to a steady glow. 'Thank you, linesmen,' she said with relief, and got to her feet, her heart thumping erratically in her chest.

The starkness of electricity should have robbed Roman of some of that lamp-lit glamour. It didn't. With every feature revealed as he stood up politely he still took her breath away with that uncompromising male beauty, both formidable and ruthless. It was intensified by the midnight hair, black lashes and brows and skin darkly tanned after his recent holiday in the sun.

A wave of desire shocked her into action. She pretended to glance at her watch. 'I'll try the telephone.'

He watched as she went across and lifted the receiver, replacing it with a frown. 'Still dead as a doornail,' she said shortly.

He finished off the shortbread and leaned back in his chair, his gaze somehow intimidating as he watched her come back to the table.

Beneath that controlled surface she was furious. Not a woman who asked for—or wanted—favours, Roman thought, fascinated by the blue sheen over her hair as she moved gracefully across the room. But he already knew that; right from the start he'd noticed her pride, as essential a part of her as the black silk of her hair, the pale skin that shimmered like water under the moon and the turbulent eyes hidden by those amazing lashes.

In the heat of passion that sleek skin had warmed to his caresses, and her eyes had blazed green fire…

Passion pierced him, sharp and urgent, painful as a goad, and spiced with the added impetus of memory. She sent him a swift, slanted glance that gleamed with an emotion he couldn't define; logic told him she was still in shock, and he wondered if he should stay rather than fly back tonight.

He dismissed the idea and asked deliberately, 'So, are you still planning to leave?'

Giselle's face closed into a pale, still mask. 'Will you really sack Joe and Rangi?'

'Yes.'

Her green eyes narrowed slightly. 'Why are you being so impossible? Punishment for daring to walk out on you?'

'I am not so petty. I want you to stay, and because I am now the owner,' he said coolly, 'I will use whatever tools I have to see that you do.'

Heat burned her face, emphasising the framework beneath the exquisite skin. Roman thought irrelevantly that those strong bones would always give her beauty, even in old age.

What the *hell* had gone wrong between them? His determination to find out surprised him. Difficult and prickly as she could be, he should have been glad to see her go.

Instead, here he was in the back of beyond where he was most emphatically not welcome.

Not now, he thought grimly, but very soon, she'd tell him. He knew what it was like to be on his own, reliant on meagre resources. His father had been no businessman; he'd spent the money his wife had earned with a recklessness that had something driven and desperate to it, so that Roman had grown up in what he could only describe as genteel poverty. His parents' deaths had left him without resources, knowing that he had no one but himself to rely on to keep him and his brother from starving.

He'd more than managed that; he'd fought his way to the top. However, it was different for women, especially beautiful, inexperienced ones; the world was full of predators. His security department had good contacts in New Zealand, and through them he knew that, once back taxes had been paid and outstanding debts settled, Giselle and her sister would get practically nothing.

And although he'd been called ruthless often enough, he wasn't heartless. She didn't know it, but she needed a breathing space.

He watched her turn his ultimatum over in her mind, trying to find a way out.

Common sense told Giselle that as head of a huge organisation as well as being Lord of the Sea Isles, Roman wouldn't be in New Zealand often.

If she stayed on, the workers would have six months to find other jobs, or establish their position at Parirua under the new regime. And eventually this foolish headstrong longing would collapse into ashes and she'd be whole again, able to function properly in the new life she'd make for herself.

She said abruptly, 'All right, then. I'll do it.'

Without emotion he said, 'So that is that. I'll leave now, but I'll be back soon; can you show me the way to Joe Watene's house, please?'

Giselle almost asked him what he wanted there, but of course she had no right to question him. As he'd pointed out so bluntly, he was now the owner; what he said went.

So she indicated the way, and then moved around the kitchen tidying and washing the dishes, her mind in such turmoil she hardly knew what she was thinking.

Ten minutes later Roman was back, this time accompanied by Joe's wife. 'Marie has agreed to stay the night with you,' he said without emotion.

'I don't need—'

He lifted one ironic brow. 'Probably not, but she is happy to do this for you.'

At Marie's nod Giselle said politely, 'Thanks, Marie.' Good manners drove her to finish, 'I'll see you down to the beach.'

Roman dismissed the suggestion with a brief shake of his head. 'I can find my own way. Goodnight.' He included Marie in his farewell and left, walking silently into the night.

Both women waited until he was out of sight, then Giselle closed the door.

Marie smiled and rolled her eyes. 'So that's the new owner! Oh, wow!'

Giselle forced a smile. 'Indeed.'

'Well, he looks like being a good boss. He thought you might need company tonight, which is why I'm here.'

Giselle said uncertainly, 'That was nice of him—not that I want to drag you out of your own bed!'

'Ah, it'll do Joe good to have to look after the baby if she wakes,' Marie said comfortably.

The noise of the chopper's engines silenced them; both women fell silent until it took off. When the sound had faded Marie said, 'OK, show me the bedroom you want me to use and I'll make up a bed in it.'

Later, lying awake in her lonely bed, Giselle was glad there was another person in the house. The thought showed an unexpectedly kind side of Roman Magnati.

But it didn't alter the fact that he'd used Joe and Rangi as bargaining tools.

The homestead had been a refuge to her, free of Roman's presence. No longer; he'd walked in the door and stamped his dominant, uncompromising magnetism on the place as if it had always belonged to him.

CHAPTER NINE

AFTER Marie had left the next morning to get breakfast for her family, Giselle rang Leola and told her who owned the organisation that had bought Parirua.

And waited anxiously for her sister's response.

It came after a taut few seconds. 'I see,' Leola said, so guardedly that Giselle knew her suspicions had some foundation. 'Seems rather coincidental that you met him in Fala'isi, doesn't it?'

Giselle said, 'Oh, you know New Zealand—stand on any street corner and you're bound to meet someone you know. The South Pacific is obviously the same.' And steered the conversation into safer grounds. 'Where did the prince get all this money? I thought his father left Illyria with nothing.'

'They're a family of over-achievers.' Leola's voice echoed hers—brittle and bright. 'And, yes, Prince Roman's father fled the country empty-handed.'

'Except for a Swiss bank account packed with money, perhaps.'

'Oh, don't be so cynical.' Leola paused, then said sharply, 'He really did get to you, didn't he?'

You don't know how much, Giselle thought in weary disillusion. 'I wouldn't like anyone who bought Parirua.'

Leola gave a constrained laugh. 'No, you wouldn't. I'm still feeling a bit weepy about losing it myself. But I think you're probably too pessimistic to believe he's going to fill Parirua with tatty mock-Mediterranean villas. Why don't you ask him his plans?'

'Because it's none of my business,' Giselle said grittily. 'We sold it to him, remember?'

'You're being stubborn. Wouldn't it make you happier if you knew he wasn't going to ruin the place?'

'Well—oh, yes, of course it would.' It was a lie. A partial one, anyway. She hated the fact that she and her sister were talking across each other, choosing their words, treading gently. It was the first time it had happened; even when they'd fought they'd always been open with each other.

Leola said, 'From the little I've seen of the Considine-Magnati family they have taste. Besides, he must realise that Parirua isn't suited to being turned into a suburb, even a seaside suburb.'

'I wish Prince Alex had made a better job of calling all his freeloading relatives back to Illyria,' Giselle burst out, then caught herself up.

Leola said crisply, 'Can you call tycoons freeloaders? And the Illyrians need as much help as they can get. Things are moving for them, but their ruler has warned them it'll take years before they can expect much return on their hard work. They're pushing health and education first.'

'Sounds sensible.' Mouth dry, Giselle probed, 'You seem to know a lot about Illyria's problems. When did you meet Roman Magnati?'

Her heart skidded into overdrive as Leola hesitated, but her reply was delivered in her most offhand voice. 'Oh, a while ago I had a couple of dates with a man who moved in the same circles.' Abruptly her sister changed tack. 'I have to admit it's a bit of a blow to find out just how little money there's left now everything's paid up.' She gave a humourless little laugh. 'Pity we don't have some of the Considine/Magnati ruthlessness!'

'Indeed.' Giselle tried to soften the bald answer by adding, 'If it's any help—'

'Stop right there!' Leola interrupted indignantly, then laughed. 'You need it more than I do; I can wait a few more years before I set up on my own.'

But Giselle, still keenly attuned to every nuance in her sister's words, knew it was a real disappointment. Her heart clamped. Leola was a brilliant designer; she'd worked ferociously hard and grabbed every opportunity, and she deserved to succeed.

Before she had time to say anything, Leola resumed, 'And even though we're not going to get much out of the sale, I'm glad it's gone through.'

'*I'm* glad someone is!'

'Oh, come on, Ellie! It was no life for you and you know it. I know you love Parirua, but you just fell into staying on it because Dad needed someone to look after him and I was too selfish to do it.'

The childhood nickname tempered Giselle's bleak mood. 'Rubbish. You did what you were born to do. And don't call me Ellie…Lollie!'

'If you ever say that in front of anyone else I'll kill you,' Leola threatened. 'Lollie and Ellie—what were our parents thinking?'

'Not a lot.'

A muffled snort of laughter from the other end indicated her sister's agreement. 'If at all,' Leola said. They were both silent for a few seconds, thinking of that doomed marriage, until Leola resumed in her firmest voice, 'Don't worry about me. I'll be fine. But you take care of yourself.'

With equal determination, Giselle said, 'I won't worry about you if you promise not to worry about me. I've got six months' breathing space to find another job. I'll do it.'

The next day Giselle was drafting cattle when the sound of a helicopter's engines swooping over the hills spooked one of the calves. Bawling nervously, it raced off from the mob, and within seconds she was trying to impose control on an unruly herd of cows intent on breaking free with their offspring.

Her horse was experienced, as were the dogs, but by the time the chopper pilot got out of the way she was hot, covered in mud splashes, and seething with fury.

It took her half an hour to get the herd back together again. Still fuming, she closed the gate behind her and rode down the hill to the homestead. Roman was early.

That morning she'd had a call from a man who told her he was PA to Roman Magnati—*Prince* Roman Magnati.

'The prince will be arriving around two in the afternoon,' he'd told her. 'He wants you to be ready to take him over the station.'

'We've only got an old ute. I doubt if he'd enjoy a ride in that,' she said, fighting back a very suspect surge of adrenalin. In her most deadpan voice she added, 'Of course I could take him pillion on the quad bike, or if he doesn't mind riding a horse I have a nice old gelding here that might be suitable.'

There was a pregnant pause before the PA said thoughtfully, 'He is a superb rider, but time is part of the equation. You'd better use the ute.'

So now she was late, but that was Roman's fault. If he was going to have anything to do with Parirua while it was a working station, he'd have to learn that flying low meant trouble amongst the stock.

Then she thought of the ute, and her bad humour eased. Though perhaps she should have cleaned it up a bit. Even in casual clothes Roman looked like someone out of a fantasy—very exclusive, very self-sufficient, his aura of authority uncompromised. It would be interesting to see how he dealt with a truck that had seen its best days a generation ago.

He was already at the house, sitting in one of the ancient wicker chairs on the veranda. When Giselle came around the corner he put down the papers he'd been reading and got to his feet, his potent male charisma, based on that unique combination of stunning good looks and compelling control, very much in evidence.

Her heart lurched, and something tightened deep inside her, a powerful tug of attraction that was a mixture of excitement and anticipation tinged by the bitter tang of betrayal. Had she misjudged him?

Each time she asked herself this, she had to face the fact that Leola had been extremely guarded when she'd spoken of him—hiding her emotions in a way that wasn't usual for her.

'Good afternoon,' she said evenly, not smiling. 'Do you usually fly low enough to terrify any animals unfortunate enough to be in your vicinity?'

She'd planned to be showered and clean before he'd arrived. Now clad in mud-spattered jeans and a T-shirt dating back to her high-school days, she felt at even more of a disadvantage.

Coolly Roman said, 'That was a mistake by the pilot. It won't happen again.'

She looked around. 'Where is he?'

'In the chopper checking the rules.' He surveyed her face with unreadable eyes.

In her most remote voice she asked, 'Can I get you and him a cup of coffee? I need to shower.'

'I'll have one. He has a Thermos, I believe. I'll see to the coffee while you change.' When she hesitated he gave her a thin smile. 'I watched you make it last time.'

Reluctantly she nodded and led the way into the house, wishing he could have seen it when her mother had been in charge. Then it had been gracious and welcoming, always full of guests, the rooms smelling of the special pot-pourri she'd culled from the garden.

Sometimes Giselle wondered if her mother had been trying to make over the place she saw as a prison. Now the house both looked and felt neglected. Would he demolish it?

An hour later they were driving slowly along the central race, the road that connected every paddock. The overnight showers had cleared, but the race was still muddy so Giselle was driving with care.

They'd almost reached the highest point when the vehicle lurched and clattered. 'Damn!' Giselle muttered, wrestling with the wheel.

'Puncture?' Roman asked as she brought the vehicle to a halt.

'Yes.' She switched off the engine.

He opened the door and got out. 'Where is the jack?'

Surprised, Giselle said, 'I'll get it.' She groped under the vacated seat and hauled out the tool.

'Give it to me,' Roman said from just above her.

She looked up, saw his face far too close to hers, and had to stop herself from leaning towards him. 'It's all right,' she told him curtly.

His mouth hardened. 'Give it to me,' he repeated, and

the iron note of command in his voice startled her into loosening her grip on the jack. He took it from her unwilling hands and stepped back.

Heart thumping unevenly, she got out and went to the rear of the vehicle to examine the tyre. It had blown completely. Damn, she thought, damn, damn, *damn*! Why now?

And quite unfairly she found herself blaming the man who was squatting to fit the jack into place.

'I can do that,' she said curtly.

Raising a black brow, he said, 'Don't be foolish.'

Giselle tried again. 'You'll get dirty—there's mud everywhere. Believe me, I know what to do—I've done it several times before.'

She stopped as he stood up, but he didn't back off. Instead he swiftly undid his shirt. 'If the thought of my getting dirty concerns you so much, you can hold this.' He tossed it at her before getting back to work.

Giselle blinked. Colour flooded her face and she turned away to thrust the garment, warm from his body, onto the front seat as though it contaminated her.

Turning back, she swallowed. His bronzed torso gleamed in the sunlight, long muscles shifting and flexing smoothly as he pumped the jack.

Her breath lodged in her throat. In the time they'd spent at Flying Fish she'd seen him naked often enough, so she had no reason to feel as though something had hollowed out her stomach.

Horrified by the rush of adrenalin surging through her, she tried to shrug off the dangerous impact he was having on her too-susceptible body. Yes, Roman was strong, and he knew what he was doing.

Big deal, she thought staunchly, swallowing hard

because her throat felt as though something—her heart?—had lodged in it. Joe was nowhere near as big, but he was probably stronger; he was also competent, but she didn't go into meltdown whenever she saw him without his shirt.

Because she didn't want Joe. Because her stupid mind wasn't cluttered with memories of him in her arms…

Furious with herself, she bent to get the spare wheel from under the tray. Thank heavens Roman hadn't noticed her unguarded reaction to all his vital male potency.

Roman ordered, 'Leave it.'

'I can do it,' she said between her teeth, and unscrewed the nuts holding the wheel in place.

She dragged it out and set it against the side of the ute, angry with him and frustrated because in spite of everything that had happened she was literally aching with unsatisfied longing.

Once she'd read that every woman fell a little in love with the first man she made love to. She hadn't believed it but now—now she suspected it might be right, and the thought terrified her.

Roman changed the wheel efficiently and stood up, looking down at the shredded tyre. 'This was dangerous,' he said brusquely. 'It's bald. It should have been replaced months—possibly years—ago.'

Stiffening, Giselle returned with frigid politeness, 'Thank you for changing it.' Then, ashamed by her lack of grace, she added, 'It took considerably less time than I'd have been able to manage it in.'

She kept her eyes on the discarded wheel, refusing to look at his bare chest and the broad shoulders that sloped down to narrow hips.

Roman stooped to pick up the discarded wheel and sling it onto the tray of the ute, moving with the lithe male grace that figured so largely in her dreams. Fiery and demanding, hunger surged through her.

'I've got wipes inside the cab,' she said hoarsely, and grabbed the packet from the front shelf, taking one before handing it to him.

He cleaned his long fingers before shrugging back into his shirt. Relieved, Giselle scrambled behind the wheel and they set off again for the airstrip.

Once there she indicated the various paddocks, the landforms and the buildings. He asked a few pointed questions that had her scrambling to answer, and some that made her blink. Regardless of whether he knew anything about farming, he appeared to have a good understanding of Northland's soils and geology.

She wondered whether the evidence of chronic lack of finance was as obvious to him as it was to her. For ten years little money had been available for even basic repairs and maintenance, and nothing for new development.

Of course, she thought with another twist of anger, Roman wasn't planning to farm it; he wanted to cover it in houses.

As they came down the last hill towards the homestead he said, 'I intend to fly over the station now. It would help if you came with me and pointed out the boundaries.'

'I'll come if you make sure the pilot keeps high enough so the noise doesn't spook the cattle,' she said tartly, oddly disconcerted. He could have ordered her to come with him.

'He will.' He smiled down at her, and her stupid heart began to race. 'I'm sorry about that. He's from the city.'

Giselle shrugged, bitterly resenting the effect of that killer smile. 'Cows with calves at heel are always flighty.'

Half an hour later she stared down from the chopper, her face bleak. From the air she could see with cold, heartbreaking clarity what needed to be done on the station. Every sin and omission of the past years was spread out before her. She and her father had kept Parirua going, but only just.

Mortified, Giselle closed her eyes to hide the angry sheen of her tears, and when she opened them again they met Roman's dark ones, cool and intent and calculating. She turned away, but she suspected he knew what had been going through her head.

The station was sliding into wilderness, its paddocks full of weeds because most of the money had been spent keeping the animals healthy and paying the farm workers. Fences were failing, buildings needed renovation, and the grass showed years of under-fertilisation.

Back at the homestead Roman said calmly, 'So tell me what has happened here.'

Pride stinging, she said in a low, tight voice, 'When my mother and my father divorced, under New Zealand law she was entitled to half his assets. My father had just bought Parirua from my grandfather, so he had no ready money. Between them Dad and Grandad cashed up every investment, everything they had, but Dad still had to mortgage Parirua to pay my mother her share. It happened at just the wrong time; we had several bad years after that and by the time things improved it was too late for Parirua.'

'Why didn't your father sell the station?'

'Because he was born here,' she said simply. 'So were his father and grandfather and great-grandfather.' She added with a twist of her lips, 'You should understand that.'

One black brow lifted in acknowledgement of the hit. 'Perhaps I do. At the moment you're angry, and perhaps a bit scared of what will happen to you, but tell me this—how much longer do you think you could have held on?'

Unerringly, he'd found the secret fear that had kept her awake too many nights over the past few years. 'Don't you dare presume to tell me what's best for me. You can't have any understanding of what losing Parirua means,' she flashed. He was a pirate, picking up loot from the wreckage. She added cuttingly, 'After all, you barely know me.'

'Oh, I feel I know most of the important things about you,' he said in a low, dangerous voice, and before she had time to move he'd caught her in his arms and kissed her, a blatant act of power meant to intimidate and arouse.

It did both.

Sheer fury at her own pathetic lack of resistance drove Giselle to ball her fist and aim it at his midriff, but the sheet of solid muscle there rendered her blow harmless, and before she had a chance to repeat it the potent magic of his mouth on hers shocked her into subjection.

A passionate craving possessed her, stark and exhilarating, terrifying yet completely familiar. Her brain shut down.

When he lifted his head a fraction she realised that she was clinging to him, moulded against the hardness of his aroused body, and that the whimpering sounds she could dimly hear were coming from her. His hands across her back were gentle, but the impact of his kiss left her speechless and dazed, as though it had been a blow rather than a caress.

He trailed soft kisses across to her ear lobe, and bit it gently. Fire swept through every nerve fibre, fierce and exhilarating and mindless.

She felt his chest lift against her tingling, aching breasts, and realised that he was laughing, low and deep and triumphant.

She jerked her head back, met eyes that smouldered like midnight fire. 'And you know me—a little,' he said quietly, his mouth so close to her lips that she could feel the words against her sensitised flesh. 'But not as well as you will.'

It was a threat, not a promise.

Bitter pride displaced the headstrong tide of desire. Wrenching herself free, she said unevenly, 'I will not, because I won't be around to be used like a plaything. I'm leaving, Mr Magnati—or do I call you Your Highness?'

A black brow rose to chilling effect. 'You do not call me anything other than my given name—the title is reserved for the people of Illyria who wish to use it. And I must remind you—again—that you are contractually bound to stay here for six months. This continuous threatening to leave is becoming tiresome.'

Cornered, she met his implacable eyes, cold and stony. The handsome features were forbidding, a mask of power and relentless determination, and she accepted with stinging frustration that she had no way out.

'All right, you win,' she said bleakly. 'But don't ever touch me again. If you do, I'll sue you for sexual harassment. We have laws against that in New Zealand, and I'm sure you wouldn't want to figure in a humiliating court case.'

Dark eyes hooded, he gave one of those swift, Mediterranean shrugs. 'You have made your feelings more than clear. Be assured, I won't touch you again unless you beg me to.'

It would be a cold day in hell before she fell that low! She said proudly, 'Then that's all right.'

'Now that that's out of the way,' he said, dismissing the previous few minutes as though they'd never existed, 'I have the plans for you to look at.'

'Plans? What plans?'

'The plans for development. Merely rough sketches at the moment, but they give a fair idea of how I see the future of Parirua.'

'I don't want to see them.' Her voice sounded thick and impeded. She coughed and started again. 'All I'm interested in is the next six months. I assume I'll get my orders from someone who knows what they're doing when it comes to pastoral farming in Northland.'

Six months stretched before her like centuries.

She had to last out that long, and after that she'd never see him again.

'If he doesn't at first, I'm sure you'll tell him all about it,' Roman said courteously.

CHAPTER TEN

'AND now,' Roman said in a voice that was all dominant command, 'I wish to show you the plans. Is there a dining room here, or some place where we can spread them out on a table?'

Woodenly Giselle replied, 'Of course,' and walked out of the room, every inch of her skin tightening as he noiselessly followed her. The wide hall with its familiar family acquisitions looked—and smelt—run-down and shabby, she admitted in a moment of searing, painful honesty.

Roman's compelling, vital personality stripped away the years when her family had owned the house and the land, stamping everything with his complex, ruthless presence.

Pushing open the door into the dining room, she wondered how it was possible to want somebody as much as you resented him.

At least he didn't gloat. He'd routed her comprehensively, but that intimidating authority was leashed by his will when he spread the plans out on the huge Victorian table. At first she was so painfully aware of him beside her she could barely make out the lines and colours, but fierce blinking helped clear her vision.

'It will be a farm development,' he said coolly, and indicated a big area of steep hill country. 'This land should never have been converted into pasture. It's eroding badly, so it will be returned to bush and covenanted to provide for its safety.'

She bit her lip. Against local advice and ignoring her pleas, her father had insisted on cutting down the bush on those precipitous faces.

'Parirua will work very well as a stud farm, I am advised,' Roman said.

'Do you know anything about stud cattle?' she asked sceptically.

'A little.' He added with a negligent shrug, 'But I can afford the best advice. And the best manager.'

Stung at being put so firmly in her place, Giselle resumed her examination. The race system was to be upgraded into a road that led to house sites. She made a rapid count: twenty-three.

'They have been chosen for views and amenities and privacy,' Roman told her. 'The homestead will be repaired and restored and used as the manager's residence, but the workers' houses are beyond saving; they will be replaced.'

The hard knot at the centre of Giselle's chest eased. It could have been so much worse.

Coldly, reluctantly, she said, 'It looks very sophisticated. Who will buy these house sites in the middle of nowhere on a farm?'

'That will be no problem,' he told her with clinical detachment. 'They will sell to people who want privacy and a connection to the land—people who intend to live here mostly, although some will only come for holidays.'

She pointed at one particular spot. 'You'll have to change this—it's a *urupa*. A sacred site,' she translated. 'Centuries ago a battle was fought there; the ground is tapu and any attempt to put a road through it will be fought vigorously by both the local *iwi*—tribe—and the Historic Places Trust.'

Frowning, he leaned over to look at it. She edged back, her turbulent pulse thundering in her ears. For a second his scent—erotic, pure male, hauntingly familiar—taunted her with his closeness.

'I see.' He straightened up to go on smoothly, 'You are going to be very useful to this project.'

'How?' she asked, wary and suspicious.

'Local knowledge. You know where the protected sites are, and I understand you're on excellent terms with the local Maori who have an input into the process.'

'That won't make any difference. If they disapprove of your plans they'll object, no matter that I went to school with their children. And they would dislike you instantly if they knew you'd used Joe and Rangi as levers to make me stay.' She met his eyes, her own furiously green. 'But then—you're an expert in making use of people, aren't you?'

'I do whatever is necessary.' The words, delivered almost softly, sounded ominously like a warning, a warning reinforced by the cold, unsparing relentlessness she saw in his arrogant features.

'Indeed you do,' Giselle said just as quietly, not giving an inch.

'Remember that.'

'I'm not likely to forget.' Tension sparked like wildfire between them, until she shrugged and gestured at the papers spread out on the table. 'When will all this start?'

'The negotiations with officialdom are already in progress.' Although his voice was coolly pragmatic, his eyes never left her face.

Colour tinged her skin; she fought for control, pretending to look more closely at the plans.

He went on, 'As soon as we get the go-ahead, the general overhaul of the station will begin. My project manager checked out your list, and agrees that decent roading is the first priority.'

He was establishing that although he'd just kissed her witless, from now on everything was going to be purely business. Stiffly, furious at her own inconsistency in being hurt, she objected, 'The new workers' cottages are even more important.'

'They're already under construction; in six weeks' time they'll be barged in.'

'I hope you plan to ask Marie and Lisa what they want?' she flashed.

'That will be your job. Of course you will work to a budget, and you'll liaise with the project manager and with me.'

Her head came up and she stared at him in jolting dismay. 'Why?'

'It is normal to work to a budget,' he said, brows lifting in sardonic query.

'Why do I have to liaise with both you *and* the project manager?' Colour burned the sweep of her cheekbones. Oh, why had she blurted that out?

'Because I say so,' he returned, his eyes as hard as his voice.

She had no one to blame but herself. She had, she realised with aching despair, become accustomed to some response from him, even if it was only sexual. Now that she'd threatened him he was showing her just how easy it was for him to switch from heated lust to this cold professionalism.

Every word he said, every movement he made, his effortless control, reinforced his attitude. She'd made her conditions; he'd stick to them.

Of course, for him there were always other women, whereas there would never be another man for her. And now her memories of Parirua would always be coloured by his overpowering presence.

Later, she decided; she'd deal with all this later. She demanded, 'Will the buyers realise that at times cattle are noisy and messy? That aerial topdressing starts at dawn and goes on until dusk? That haymaking is also noisy, as well as being dusty?' She pointed to one house site overlooking a river valley, heavily clad in tall bush. 'There are kiwis in this valley and they call at night—as loud and as harsh as a peacock. Are the new owners going to know they're protected birds?'

Another of those Latin shrugs, deeper this time. 'The opportunity to see the bird life return will be part of the appeal,' he said dryly, dismissing her concern. 'The Department of Conservation are eager to show us how to clear the forests of predators and return it as close to its pristine state as possible. I believe that the resulting bird chorus will be truly impressive. As well, managing the forest will bring work to the district.'

'In New Zealand we don't use the word forest like that. We call it the bush.' She straightened up, but kept her gaze on the plans.

'I stand corrected.' With a mixture of exasperation and sardonic amusement, Roman waited for the next objection.

Sure enough she said, 'What about the power supply? And the telephone? As you know, they're not reliable.'

'They will be by the time the first owner moves in,' he told her, watching that lush mouth tighten.

Time to make an end to this. She had given her word

and he was almost sure she'd keep it, but she needed to know who was master here now.

'If you're thinking of sabotage,' he advised in his most lethal tone, 'give it up.'

Giselle's head whipped up and she fixed him with blazing eyes and a haughty expression. 'I resent that. I've tried to look after Parirua,' she said jerkily. 'I wouldn't do anything to obstruct its rehabilitation.'

He let his eyes linger on her face; she met them with an indignant stare. Roman inclined his head. 'Then we'll deal very well together,' he said, and on an impulse held out his hand. 'Shall we shake on it?'

After a second's hesitation she took his hand and they shook. Her grip was firm, her skin soft, and he felt a sudden quick surge of possessiveness.

Her mouth was a dead give-away—full, passionate, unconsciously beckoning. Roman's body responded urgently as he recalled in too vivid detail the feel of it on his skin. Was she remembering too? Perhaps, because she relinquished his hand as though it had become red-hot and the flakes of colour along her cheekbones deepened before she turned away.

'So that is settled,' he said, his voice harsh. 'I have booked a table for us at the Ariki Bay resort. If you could be ready in an hour, we'll go up in the helicopter and have dinner there.'

She looked astonished and he finished, 'To seal the bargain.'

He could see her trying to find an excuse not to go, and thought with another stab of sardonic humour that it was probably good for his ego to be so comprehensively dismissed. Usually he had to fight women off, whereas Giselle couldn't have made it clearer that, although she'd been an eagerly responsive partner in his bed, that was now over.

Part of Giselle's despair and resentment at having to sell Parirua was because the place represented a safe home base to her, a refuge and an anchor. Eventually some man would convince her that there were other things in life than a run-down cattle station.

But not you, an inner voice taunted. Perhaps you're losing your touch.

Was that why he had kissed her? Because her outright rejection had wounded his pride?

Not entirely, he thought, ashamed because he'd behaved without honour. He'd never touched a woman against her will before, and that kiss had been the result of a rare loss of control, an action he wasn't prepared to examine too closely.

Of course he wanted her. Even clad in ill-fitting jeans and a baggy T-shirt, with her hair scraped back from her face and spattered by mud, she stirred something fierce and territorial in him.

Being Giselle, of course, she didn't accept the reason he'd given her. Her voice was almost aggressive as she said suspiciously, 'Are you going to make this an order?'

Giselle didn't trust the smile that curved his sculpted lips; it gave nothing away. 'If I must. You know everyone in that district, and who to trust.'

'Well—yes, but what's that got to do with anything?' And she was *not* disappointed in his blunt, pragmatic statement, she told herself angrily.

'You can smooth the path when it comes to the raft of consents that are required for any development here. I believe the mayor is your cousin.'

'A very distant cousin,' she shot back. 'And a very honest one. New Zealand is one of the least corrupt countries in the world, so who I'm related to won't make an atom of difference to your plans.'

'That's one of the reasons I do business here,' he returned, a thread of steel running through each word. 'But you'll be able to help with the nuances that outsiders tend to overlook.'

'Just because I've signed an employment contract doesn't mean you've bought me,' she returned, struggling to hide her pain. Clearly he intended to make as much use of her as he could.

'For the next six months it means exactly that.'

The words rang in her ears. She opened her mouth to refute them, but he cut her short before she got a sound out.

'I'm not an ogre, Giselle,' he said curtly. 'I know how much losing Parirua means to you. You've made it clear that whatever relationship we had is over, and I accept that, but that's no reason for us not to be friends.'

Friends? Later she'd think that that was when she totally lost hope. When her reaction to him veered wildly from wanting to haul him off to the nearest bedroom to resisting the urge to kill him, he could talk about being *friends*?

Of course that would be the civilised, sophisticated way of doing things.

She didn't feel at all sophisticated or civilised. Glancing down at herself, she said, 'I have nothing to wear.'

'You could wear the clothes you wore the other night. Think of it as a business dinner.'

In other words, she realised, she had no choice. Giselle said tonelessly, 'I—yes, all right.'

'Don't look so desperate,' he advised, his words edged with mockery. 'We'll eat, drink coffee in the bar, and then I'll drop you back here on my way to Auckland.'

Giselle opened her mouth, then closed it again. She was his employee. And she desperately wanted Joe and Rangi's jobs to be safe, and Parirua to go on into its second hundred years as a working station. Against her will, she was impressed by his plans for it.

Besides, pride insisted she show him that she could be every bit as detached as he was. 'Very well,' she said tonelessly.

The Ariki Bay resort had been built several years before to cater for millionaires but Giselle had never been there; she knew she'd feel totally out of place.

What did it matter? OK, so when she met Roman's enigmatic eyes the impact sizzled through every cell, and his touch had the power to temporarily cut off coherent thought, but, though her body might be enslaved by his potent male vitality, her mind felt nothing but contempt for him.

She got into the outfit she'd worn at Auckland, but this time she teamed the top with a pair of slim black trousers she hadn't worn for about ten years. No gloves, no jewellery...

And then she remembered the fire diamond bracelet, still pushed to the back of the safe. How the hell could she have forgotten it?

Moving quickly, she went into the study, took it from the safe, and carried it into the sitting room.

Roman looked up from the papers he was reading and got to his feet, glancing from the small box in her hand to meet her eyes.

Whatever she'd expected it wasn't a total shut-down of emotion in the angular, autocratic face. It hurt, and so did the burnished, opaque gaze with which he surveyed her.

Stung, she held out the small jewel case that held the bracelet. 'This belongs to you.'

'It is yours now.'

'I don't accept payment for sex,' she said stonily.

He didn't move. 'It was bought for you, not for sex.'

Well, two could use blackmail. 'I'm not going to accept

it.' She dragged in a breath. 'I'll send it to be auctioned for a charity.'

His eyes narrowed, but he must have seen that she was adamant, because he gave another of those shrugs and took the case from her hand, slipping it into his pocket. 'I'll do that. I probably have a wider acquaintance than you do of people prepared to spend on useless fripperies in an attempt to buy social prestige,' he said indifferently, a remark that once again underlined the difference between them.

She'd read an article about the unique gems, and the prices mentioned had made her gasp. A bracelet that looked much the same as hers—the one that Roman had bought, she hastily corrected—had sold by private treaty for much more than Parirua's worth.

'The chopper's waiting,' he said. 'Let's go.'

Dusk was falling when the helicopter settled down on the Ariki Bay landing pad with the usual flurry of rotors and noise.

Once they were in the car that waited for them, Roman said, 'I need to change, so we'll go to my quarters before dining.'

Wary and tense, Giselle looked out over a sea the colour of old pewter beneath a sky still faintly gold with sunset light. 'This is beautiful,' she said quietly. 'Is Ariki Bay one of your developments?'

He gave her a cool, speculative look that made her toes curl. 'Yes.'

The hotel was made up of a series of units, low and modern, set in gardens that were a lush mixture of New Zealand's amazing flora and species imported from the sub-tropics. The resort curved around an apricot beach hemmed by the huge, dark-foliaged pohutukawa trees that throve in the embrace of the sea. Behind the buildings and the gardens stretched the manicured slopes of a golf course, planted with trees that blended with the native bush in the gullies.

Tension tugged at her, setting her heart racing and her mind buzzing. Part of her was angrily resistant to being used so blatantly to further his business, yet another, hungry part desperately wanted to see what sort of house he'd chosen for himself.

'Welcome to my New Zealand home,' Roman said formally when they stopped under a wide portico that would shelter any guests from Northland's occasional torrential downpours.

He lived in a house of spare luxury, restrained and minimalist, with only the artworks to hint at the sort of man he was. Always providing he'd chosen them, Giselle thought snidely.

'Can I get you a drink?' he asked in the living room.

'Juice, thank you.'

He poured her lime juice, and brought it across to where she was sitting, every nerve wound tight as she tried to look relaxed and in command of herself.

'I won't be long,' he told her.

Too aware of him, she nodded and picked up the glass, sipping the chilled liquid after he'd left the room.

A distant hum told her he was probably showering. After the first time at Flying Fish they'd showered together each day, an exercise that rapidly turned into fierce love-making... Memories of the incandescent passion, the laughter and fierce desire, the feel of his sleek, strong body against her as they came together set the blood racing through her body. She gulped the cool juice down, and tried to exorcise the restless, fiery hunger by getting to her feet.

A superb oil on the wall caught her attention, a sombre, intensely painterly abstract she recognised as being by one of New Zealand's greatest artists. She went across to examine it more closely, but before she reached it a photograph caught her attention.

It showed a blue, blue sea, edged by cliffs and white beaches and a small, manmade harbour with a scattering of houses behind it. A rocky land, tawny and stark and hazed with trees that were probably olives, rose to an eminence crowned by a huge, grim castle made of stone the same sun-kissed hue as the land.

In its shadow huddled a small city, the house walls forming a defence that was reinforced by a purpose-built one. A platform bordered with ancient columns stood just outside the walls, still serene and graceful after thousands of years. A temple, she thought, and her heart quickened as though somehow she recognised it.

Whatever, she was pretty sure she knew where the photograph had been taken; this was the castle in Illyria where Roman's ancestors had lived, empowered to defend the principality from pirates and corsairs and any other raiders that had prowled the ancient Middle Sea.

Lord of the Sea Isles, she thought, and shivered, her remembered desire fading as rapidly as it had come. The photograph emphasised how different their lives were.

How many other women had Roman brought to Ariki Bay?

Who knew? she thought with mordant flippancy. But at least Leola had never been here.

A stark, intense bitterness drove her into activity. She walked out onto a terrace that faced the sea, but images of her sister and Roman together sprang too vividly into her mind.

Had he sought her out on Fala'isi because he'd known she was Leola's twin?

Although she heard nothing, she turned quickly to see

Roman come onto the terrace, his big body lithe and powerful in the black and white austerity of evening clothes. Her heart flipped and feverish little thrills sang through her.

'Do you want to walk down?' he asked coolly. 'We can take the car if you'd rather.'

Sitting in the close confines of a car with him would stretch her brittle control past breaking-point. 'I'd like to walk.'

His smile was almost a taunt, as though he'd expected her answer. 'Then let's go.'

But once back in the sitting room she stopped and looked again at the magnificent oil, then transferred her gaze to the photograph of the castle on its island.

Roman's voice startled her. 'What do you see when you look at them?'

'The picture—emotion trapped by paint, but the castle is all about naked power and influence.'

'Whereas I see beauty, and my home,' he said abruptly.

Perhaps he didn't realise how bluntly his words underlined the distance between them. No, he said nothing without reason, she thought bleakly.

And the point was well taken. She would never belong in a world where castles were taken for granted.

Giselle tried not to feel conspicuous as she walked beside him into the busy restaurant, but her height made her an easy target for speculative glances, and of course Roman attracted attention wherever he went.

Most were subtle about checking them out, but a couple of women made their interest obvious, their eyes widening when they took in his intense male potency and intangible, uncompromising air of cool self-containment. Giselle fought back a primal territorial urge to give them a look that commanded *Keep off!*

They were led to a secluded table where Roman ordered drinks—a dry white wine as an aperitif—and discussed the menu with her. When the very attentive waiter left, he raised his glass and smiled narrowly, his expression as unreadable as his eyes.

'Here's to Parirua's new incarnation,' he said.

'To Parirua,' she repeated, the words flat. Cautiously she sipped the wine. New Zealand made, it was light and young, tasting of fresh herbs. She relaxed and put her glass down.

His voice was casual as he asked, 'What does the name of the station mean?'

Surprised, she told him, '*Pari* means flowing tide, and *rua* is the Maori word for two. If you remember, about a kilometre past the homestead the harbour splits into two long inlets that run up into the hills and eventually turn into two small rivers.'

'I do remember. And your family have been living there since the area was settled by Europeans?'

'Yes. Do you plan to market it under that name?'

'Why not?' His broad shoulders lifted in a slight shrug. 'It's pretty.'

Challengingly she asked, 'If its name translated into something like Rotten Fish would you still call it Parirua?'

'Names of localities are given by the people who live in the area, not by developers. I wouldn't even try to change it.'

Giselle didn't want to find things to like about him. She filled in a few seconds by sipping more wine, then asked, 'Why did you go back to Illyria and the Sea Isles? Because it's your birthright?'

He leaned back in the chair, his indolent posture denied by the leashed power beneath the conventional armour of his evening clothes. 'When the dictator's forces overran the isles the islanders saved my father. He was only young, barely a teenager, but he'd been wounded in the fighting, and several of them smuggled him across to Italy in a fishing boat. His rescuers paid for that act of gallantry with their lives, and their families paid again and again under the dictator. My brother and I owe our very existence to them. You could say we owe them a debt of blood.' He paused, then went on, 'Also, before he died I promised my father that I'd always do what I could for them.'

Giselle hid her unwilling respect and nodded, startled by her next thought. 'So what you're doing there is an extension of this—building communities.'

'Only people can build communities; all developers do is make sure that the infrastructure is suitable for that to happen,' he said lazily, watching her with half-closed eyes. 'But, yes, I suppose my interest in development was stirred because I hoped that one day I'd be able to help in the reconstruction of the Sea Isles. I had no idea, of course, just how difficult a job it would be.'

Difficult or not, it was one he intended to finish if the jut of his angular jaw was any indication.

He looked at her and smiled. 'But you know all about fighting for a piece of land.'

Giselle drew in a sharp breath as the air suddenly turned electric. Sharp desire pierced her, bringing heat to her skin and a fierce pang of need. She stumbled for something to say, finally asking in a voice that was too husky, 'Do you live in the castle in the photograph?'

He looked amused. 'Unfortunately, yes. It's magnificently uncomfortable, but my cousin Gabriele's wife is an interior decorator and, once she's finished restoring his home in the mountains of the mainland to order and comfort, she plans to turn her attention to my ruin. She says it's even more of a challenge. I have to admit that she's transforming the Wolf's Lair into a very pleasant home without disturbing its ambience, so I'll probably give her carte blanche to do as she sees fit.'

CHAPTER ELEVEN

ROMAN looked across the candle-lit table. 'When you leave Parirua, what do you plan to do? I believe you had ambitions once to be an artist.'

He'd certainly had her checked out, Giselle thought, her sensual tension transforming into outrage. She hated the thought of someone prying into her life so intimately.

Still, that was better than the other possibility—that Leola had told him. She traced the top of her wineglass with a long finger, stopping when she noticed her fingernail—short, unpolished, and not in the least elegant.

At least it was clean, she thought sardonically, but recalling Bella Adams' softly gleaming nails on the sleeve of Roman's jacket—probably the very same evening jacket—she folded her hands in her lap.

'That was a high-school fantasy,' she told him with crisp distinctness. 'I soon realised I was never going to be as good as Felice Longfellow.'

He picked up her allusion to the painter who'd produced the masterpiece in his chalet. 'Is that a reason for giving up?'

'Yes,' she said simply. 'I like to do things properly.' She thought for a moment. 'I might study to be an accountant, actually.'

And enjoyed his startled look.

'Why?' he asked.

'Because neither my father nor my grandfather were good with money, and if you don't know how to organise your finances things go wrong. Besides, it's a nice, steady occupation.'

'You sound like my brother,' he said, clearly amused.

This time she was the one who was startled. 'Your brother is an accountant?'

'Not exactly.'

'What does he do?'

His shoulders lifted. 'He's had several occupations,' he said dryly. 'And I've no doubt that if you decide to take it up you'd make an excellent accountant. But why not study art and find out if you do have the talent to be a success?'

'I have a facile skill in drawing, but I don't think I have the talent to be a good artist. Or the passion.'

'I see,' he said, watching her. 'Yet there is passion in you.' He watched the colour storm along her cheekbones, and said smoothly, 'More passion than can be tamed by an accountancy degree, perhaps.'

Her sexual vulnerability infuriated her, but not as much as his deliberate taunt. 'At least I'll know how to cope with money,' she returned. 'As for my interest in art—I can use that to appreciate a good artist when I see their work.'

'So are you a farmer at heart?' he asked, an idle question that surprisingly struck home.

She pondered, before saying in a surprised voice, 'I think I must be.'

'Tell me, is it the loss of Parirua you mourn, or the satisfaction of producing something from the land?'

Wariness made her pause. He saw too much, this man with his midnight eyes and his brilliant brain and that uncompromising air of self-mastery. 'Both,' she said curtly. 'The family heritage is important, and, yes, I enjoy working the land. I like being outdoors, I like seeing things grow, I like applying new technology. I know it's not exactly fashionable to be a farmer, but it's what I am.'

His brows shot up. 'What has fashion to do with it? Don't you believe there is such a thing as a vocation?'

Leola had designed and made clothes as soon as her fingers were long enough to hold scissors, whereas Giselle had always been the tomboy. 'Of course,' she said with a shrug, and turned the subject with a total lack of finesse. 'How are farm parks organised legally?'

He told her, eyes veiled by his lashes as he surveyed her slightly down-bent face—the clear, translucent skin he found so desirable, the determined jaw, the clean, sleek lines of her. His body hardened and he wanted her with a proprietorial craving that startled him with its elemental, erotic charge.

She wasn't looking at him, but he knew her whole attention was concentrated on him—because they were talking about her beloved Parirua. He wished he knew what was going on behind that maddeningly self-possessed face.

Why was he so intrigued by her? Lust was simple, a physical response he could usually control. And normally he didn't waste time on difficult women.

He hadn't been very old when he'd realised that even a defunct title was touched by magic for many women, especially when it was combined with dark good looks. His rapid acquisition of a fortune only added to his appeal. After a couple of unsatisfactory affairs he'd developed a thick hide and a cool cynicism that had kept him safe from the wilder shores of sexuality, until Giselle—with her pale skin and eyes of green witchery, her lush mouth and convenient sense of responsibility to the people who worked for her and the land she'd owned—had goaded him into indiscretion.

He finished curtly, 'If you need to know more, ask.'

Later, when they moved into the bar for coffee, Giselle smiled across at the father of a school friend, the councillor for their particular district, and wasn't much surprised when he came across. Bitterly recalling the reason Roman had brought her to Ariki Bay, she introduced them.

She listened to the subsequent conversation with growing admiration for Roman's acute intelligence; she knew the councillor well enough to realise that he too was impressed, and before he went back to his group the two men set up a meeting.

'It looks as though bringing me here *was* a good move on your part,' she said with pointed sarcasm.

Roman didn't pretend not to know what she was referring to. 'Developers—sensible developers—learn very early that the most important element for a successful development is keeping the local people in the picture.'

'He seemed very interested.'

'It's in his interest to be aware of anything that might help his chances of being re-elected. More work in the community makes for more services, more taxes, and more contented people.'

'You seem to know a lot about the area.'

'My people do their homework,' he said matter-of-factly. 'Any project needs a good background strategy.'

Did he run his private life with the same sort of approach? And where did Leola fit into this? Giselle wondered with a pang of nausea.

She looked down at her coffee, black and sugarless, wishing it were some nostrum that would stop the constant treadmill of her thoughts. Roman's motives didn't matter.

From the start she'd known there was no future for them, yet she'd chosen to make love with him. And though he'd certainly been attracted, he wouldn't have made a move if she hadn't given all the right signals.

With women like Bella Adams in his life, why would he want a lover who had no skills but agricultural ones?

Giselle had had enough of struggling to make things work when they were irreparably broken. In spite of all her efforts, Parirua was no longer hers. It wasn't her fault, and she'd had to grit her teeth and accept the situation.

She could do the same with this foolish yearning. Look on it as an educational experience, she advised herself stringently. Learn from it; enjoy the good memories, banish the bad.

With mordant self-derision she decided she was starting to sound like a self-help book.

Too lightly, she said, 'That tall thin man with receding red hair is a building contractor. He's good, and he's honest. You *are* planning to use locals, aren't you?'

'Wherever I can,' Roman told her.

'Do you want me to smile at him?' Her tone coloured the question with sardonic inflection.

'Perhaps a wave of the hand,' he suggested with a dangerous smile.

The building contractor took her wave as encouragement to come across, and again the two men talked. Apparently that was enough, for after the contractor had rejoined his group Roman said, 'Time to go.'

Obediently Giselle got to her feet. The bar quietened as they headed towards the door; very aware of the covert interest, she wished fiercely that she matched him in poise and sophistication.

She probably looked utterly down-market, she thought

derisively, but what was new about that? Leola was the up-market twin.

In six months' time she'd be free of his influence. Perhaps now that she'd made it so obvious she didn't want to resume their affair, she'd never see him again.

The emptiness inside her expanded into an aching desolation, one she tried to ignore on the flight back to Parirua. Once there, she was lifted out of the chopper by Roman, but he let her go immediately so that they could hurry across the beach.

When they were far enough away for her to be heard, she stopped and said, 'It's all right, you don't need to come any further.'

'I am walking you to the homestead,' he said implacably. 'We have had this argument at least twice before and I am bored with it.'

When she bared her teeth at him he laughed, low and taunting and completely self-assured. 'The sooner you move, the sooner you'll be rid of me,' he reminded her.

Abruptly she turned and walked up the path through the garden, her heartbeat drumming out the crunch of their feet on the white shell path. Shoulders and spine aching with rigidity, she turned the handle in the front door and pushed it open.

He asked sharply, 'Why isn't it locked?'

'The keys were lost years ago. It's perfectly safe. To get here you have to go past the cottages, and the dogs would let Joe or Rangi know if anyone came.'

His brows met across his arrogant nose. 'Someone could land on the beach and walk up from there.'

'There's nothing worth stealing here.'

'I'll check out the house.'

Exasperated now, she said curtly, 'It's all right, I tell you!'

He came across the threshold, putting her quite gently to one side. 'I will check out the house, and then I'll go.'

But his hands on her arms tightened, and she swayed towards him, her body betraying her in that one involuntary movement.

She heard the hiss of his breath. 'Shall I send the pilot away?' he said in à low, rough voice. 'Are you begging, Giselle? So soon after your threats and valiant words this afternoon?'

Humiliation scorching through her, she jerked free. In a low, intense voice she demanded, 'Is this how you talk to my sister?'

Silence stretched between them, brittle with tension. Giselle held her head high and met his narrowed, lethal stare without outward flinching. She couldn't go on like this; she had to know.

He said icily, 'What the hell do you mean by that?'

But some tiny muscle in his jaw was flicking. So nauseated she was barely able to articulate the words, she said, 'Just that you were seen with her in Paris. What sort of game are you playing with us?'

A white line around his mouth, he demanded harshly, 'What sort of degenerate do you think I am? Who told you I was seen with her?'

'Something B—' Giselle stopped, seeing the promise of ruthless retribution in his crystalline gaze. She didn't owe the model anything, but Bella Adams had told the truth, and she didn't deserve to be punished for that. 'I saw a photograph of you both in a magazine. I didn't realise it was Leola because it was taken from behind, but it was, wasn't it?'

'I've met your sister,' he admitted in a low, silky tone.

'And had an affair with her.'

He said something savage in a language she didn't recognise. 'Is that the only reason you've come up with this—this insult? You saw a photograph that might have been your sister, and you believed a stupid woman whose only interest in me is my title and money? What exactly did Bella Adams say to you?'

Faced by his icy fury now that his honour had been impugned, Giselle realised on what very flimsy grounds she'd built her edifice of betrayal—a photograph that might mean nothing, and the word of a jealous woman.

And Leola's unhappiness, she reminded herself.

'That doesn't matter,' she said, steadying her voice.

'Listen to me. I first met your sister at a party I gave. She came to it as my brother's guest. Yes, I found her attractive, but as Nico's date she was automatically forbidden to me.'

Stunned, Giselle couldn't find a word to say at first. Eventually she managed, 'Your *brother*?'

'They are no longer together.' His voice was cold and implacable, every word taut with anger. 'Has she told you that she is the one who set the sale of Parirua in motion?'

In total disbelief, Giselle said, 'Leola did *what*? I don't believe you. How?'

'When we met, my brother happened to mention the Ariki Bay resort. Merely as a conversation gambit, she commented that Parirua would make a great resort too, but that it had been in the family for generations, and losing it would upset her sister. That was all. It was a comment made at a party, the sort of light, throwaway remark that fills a gap, but it aroused my curiosity. I set my project manager to see whether she was right.'

'So he snooped around to see whether or not you could turn it into a farm park,' she said stonily.

'It's called gathering information,' he said with harsh

control. 'As it was perfect for the purpose we made an offer. Which you turned down.'

'Did you know who I was at Fala'isi?'

'Not at first,' he said, his tone distant. 'I didn't really believe you were paparazzi, but I had you investigated. It revealed that you were a woman who lived, as you said, on a farm in Northland. Your sister wasn't mentioned, nor the name of the farm. I didn't make the connection, probably because by then I was intrigued enough to wonder what you'd be like in bed.'

She went white, and he paused, then went on with caustic deliberation, 'At least I made some effort to find out about you, whereas you seem to have eagerly embraced a raft of baseless assumptions. Is that why you left the hotel in Auckland? Because you believed I would seduce a woman, and then, for the sheer degenerate pleasure of it, do the same to her twin?'

She had no defences. Desperate to free herself from what she'd always known to be a forlorn love, she'd seized on Bella Adams' statement to shore up her defences.

The bitter irony of it was that it hadn't worked. In her innermost heart she'd known that he'd never stoop to behaviour like that.

He looked at her with frigid contempt. 'At first I thought you experienced. At Flying Fish your announcement that you were a virgin made me pause, but you were determined.' His voice hardened. 'And you were delightful. Then my project manager phoned me to tell me who you were, and that local rumours suggested that you owed such a huge amount of back taxes you'd have to sell Parirua to cover the amount.'

'But only Joe knew.' She fired up in Joe's defence. 'He wouldn't tell anyone!'

'He didn't. One of his children apparently heard him talking to you on the phone,' Roman said coolly. 'She discussed it at school, and of course it soon swept the district.'

Scarlet flooded her face, fading abruptly into pallor. 'I see,' she said on a bleak note of resignation.

With a savage twist of his lips he asked, 'Did you ever wonder why I didn't take you back to Coconut Bay resort when I discovered that you were a virgin?'

'Of course I did. When I found out you'd bought the station, I also wondered whether you'd seen a chance of making sure that I'd sell to you.'

'If you were a man I'd strike you to the ground for saying that,' he declared furiously. 'I am no male prostitute, using what was between us to cheat you into selling.'

She flinched. 'I know that. You've just told me you didn't know who I was, and I believe you.'

'It's too late for such a touching act of faith.' He spoke with biting disdain, as though he couldn't bear to be in the same room as her. 'I left you on Fala'isi because it was dishonourable to conduct an affair with you when I was also trying to buy Parirua. For the same reason, I didn't contact you until after Parirua had been sold. I came to Auckland because I knew how you'd feel about losing the place. Foolishly, I thought I might be able to console you.'

Hot-cheeked, no longer able to think coherently, she stammered, 'I—it just seemed—I mean, I know I'm not like—well, even Leola, much less Bella Adams.'

'Of course you're not. So what has that to do with anything?'

'You sent me the bracelet as if you were paying me for a night in your bed,' she accused fiercely.

'Because you walked out on me! I admit it, I was angry—stupidly angry—but nowhere near as angry as I am

now. Your insulting accusations tell me what you really
think of me—that I'm some continental debauchee with a
kink about twin sisters. Rest assured, you'll no longer be
forced to bear my presence. I wish you happiness and pros-
perity, and that we never meet again.'

He turned on his heel and swung down the path, leaving
her standing with her hand pressed over her heart, unable to
do anything but watch him stride silently into the darkness.

She was still there when Joe appeared. 'Got a call from
the boss,' he explained worriedly. 'Have to check the house
out. He said you'd want company again tonight, so—'

'I don't need company,' she said in a brittle voice, unable
to think of anything more than that Roman was still there.
The chopper hadn't moved.

But it lifted after Joe had made a quick tour through the
house and gone down to indicate to the helicopter's occu-
pants that all was well.

He came back, called 'Goodnight,' and went on to his
house.

Slowly, with a deep, shuddering breath, she closed the
door. It had never occurred to her that Leola might have
been interested in Roman's *brother*, Nico Magnati.

'Because all you can think about is Roman,' she said
into the empty darkness.

Well, she'd got what she'd thought she wanted—she was
never going to see him again. The knowledge ached through
her while she prepared for bed and climbed in. He had gone.

She said staunchly, 'It's going to be all right,' but as she
lay there and watched the stars circle the heavens she knew
her suspicion had smirched something that might have
been rare and precious.

Insecurity, she thought, bewildered. It didn't surprise her
that Leola should date a prince, but she'd been astounded

when it seemed that Roman might have even a purely sexual interest in *her*.

Somehow, without realising it, she'd grown up with a vague, inchoate sense of inferiority.

Dry-eyed and feeling as though she'd been beaten, she tried to tell herself that she'd lost nothing. Roman had wanted her—yes, but on its own that meant little. He'd never given her any indication that he was at all serious.

And she wanted much, much more from him than a wild, torrid affair.

Finally she slid into a restless sleep harried by dark dreams, sleep that was eventually broken by the imperative shrill of the telephone. Fumbling for the receiver, she picked it up and croaked eagerly, 'Yes?'

'Giselle, is that you?'

She searched for a name to go with the voice, finally coming up with a school friend who was now a journalist for one of the big dailies. 'Peta?' she asked incredulously. 'What's the matter?'

'You know Prince Roman of Illyria, don't you? You were seen having dinner with him at Ariki Bay earlier tonight, and I was told he'd bought your station? Is that right?'

'I—yes.' It wasn't a secret. She demanded sharply, 'Why do you want to know?'

'Well, this will be a shock I'm afraid, but his helicopter's gone down somewhere on its way to Auckland.' She paused, but Giselle's throat had closed and she was unable to speak. Peta went on, 'They're about an hour overdue. There was no call for help or indication that anything had gone wrong. They think the chopper was somewhere over the hills when it went missing. They're out searching, of course. It could be just a communications malfunction, but if it was that they should have heard from them by now.'

'Thank you,' Giselle said dully and hung up. After a few seconds it burst into another shrill summons, but she kept walking towards the kitchen. 'The radio,' she said out loud, and reached for it, always kept tuned to the news station.

Her finger was almost on it when she whispered, 'No,' and sat down abruptly at the table. If she turned it on, and actually heard it confirmed—

'No,' she said again, more fiercely. Roman wasn't dead. She'd know if he was. Just as she always knew if Leola was ill or miserable, she'd feel it if he'd come to any harm.

Surely?

How long she sat there she didn't know, but she was still huddled in the chair when the sound of a helicopter's rotors broke the silence of early dawn. Terror gripping her, she got up and walked out of the house into the dim morning in time to see it land behind the pohutukawas.

The dogs' barking brought her to herself; she looked down, caught a glimpse of very elderly pyjamas, and raced inside, shedding them to haul on jeans and a shirt.

Then she ran out and down to the beach, her heart thumping so loudly she didn't hear her name the first time it was said.

'Giselle.'

Slowly she turned.

CHAPTER TWELVE

A MAN'S voice—Roman's. She gave a great sob and ran the final few yards, hurling herself into his arms. They enfolded her with satisfying strength, and he said roughly, 'It's all right! My sweet girl, it's all right. I'm fine, and so is the pilot.'

Giselle no longer cared that he didn't feel anything more for her than a transitory passion. It was enough to see for herself that he was alive.

'I knew you weren't dead,' she said into the satisfying hardness of his shoulder. 'My heart knew it—but it was so hard to convince my head.'

His arms tightened even further and she felt the kiss he dropped on her head. 'Let's go inside.'

'What about the pilot?' she asked foolishly, so overwhelmed with relief she couldn't think straight.

'He's ready to go back to Auckland—it's his wife's birthday today and he wants to be home for it.'

She looked up into his beloved face and demanded urgently, 'You're sure you're not hurt?'

'Not a bit.' His kiss proved conclusively that he was in excellent health. He lifted his head and looked at her with eyes that glittered above a challenging smile. 'It was a communications problem, not a crash. Come inside and I'll tell you about it.'

Hand in hand, they walked up through the light of a golden dawn. Once inside she scanned him again, relaxing when he gave her another smile, so slow and wicked it sent another surge of invigorating relief through her.

Swallowing back foolish tears, she pulled away and filled the kettle, asking over her shoulder, 'What happened?'

He got the coffee down from the cupboard as though he'd done it hundreds of time before. 'We were crossing the ranges, heading north because I'd decided to turn back, when the communications system died. Since we had to contact base to file an amended flight plan, we landed beside a farmhouse in a valley.'

She swung around, searching his face. 'That must have been dangerous in the dark!'

'It was brilliant moonlight,' he said soothingly. 'Unfortunately, the people who owned the house weren't there. I broke in, but their sole link to the outside world was a cell phone—which, of course, they'd taken with them when they left.' He watched her plug the kettle in and went on dryly, 'I walked some kilometres to the next house while the pilot tried to fix the system. Fortunately the neighbours were at home. They let me ring through, and then drove me back to the first house.'

'You could have rung me,' she said quietly, wondering if she was taking too much for granted. He had come back and he had kissed her—but that might not mean what she hoped.

In a harder voice he said, 'I wish I had, but it didn't occur to me that someone at base had already alerted the press. Is that how you found out?'

Flushing at the memory of her cowardice, she spooned some coffee into the pot. 'No. A school friend—she's a hotshot journo now—rang me; she'd found out we'd had dinner at Ariki Bay and I suppose she wanted to interview me.'

When Roman said something low and fierce, she smiled shakily. 'It's all right—I hung up on her, but I couldn't turn on the radio. I was too scared.'

'Scared? You?' He gave a short laugh, then said in a controlled voice, 'I would give anything to cancel my intemperate words before I left.'

Incredulously, she recalled what he'd said a few moments ago—that he'd told the pilot to turn back. A tiny flicker of hope began to burn deep inside. Without looking at him she said, 'You had reason. I did jump to conclusions.'

'Yes, you did,' he agreed. 'However, as we were flying south I mastered my anger and began to use my brain. Why on earth do you believe your sister to be the most beautiful, the most desirable, the most gifted of you two?'

'I—that's not entirely—' she said warily.

'It is true,' he interrupted, his eyes intent and penetrating. 'And it is wrong. Your sister is a very attractive woman. So are you—and you can't deny that, because feature by feature you are identical. She is vibrant and amusing and good at what she does. So are you. But I cannot see her working her heart out, exhausting her body and strength to keep Parirua going as you have done.'

'She would have if she'd had to.'

He shrugged. 'Possibly. But she is not lovelier than you, nor is she more gifted. Someone once said that comparisons are odious; it is true. You are yourself, a woman with every bit as much to offer the world as your sister.' And then, dismissing Leola, he said, 'So where do we go from here, Giselle?'

'I don't know,' she said quietly. *Wherever you want to go...*

'Look at me.'

It was a command, delivered in a tone that lifted the hair on the back of her neck. Heart thudding unevenly, she finished pouring water into the coffee-pot and set the kettle down before turning.

He looked taut, tanned skin drawn over the superb framework of his face, his eyes burnished and unreadable. 'I want you to marry me,' he said, then made an abrupt gesture. 'No, that is not right. Giselle, I love you. Will you marry me?'

This time she didn't blink the tears back. Whatever she'd expected it wasn't this. Weakly, she let herself feel the intense joy of the moment, until common sense took over. 'Thank you,' she said simply, 'but no. It wouldn't work out.'

His chin came up. 'What exactly do you mean by that?' he asked, his lips barely moving.

Giselle thought she saw a long line of autocratic ancestors, Lords of the Sea Isles, move into ghostly position behind him, ready for battle.

With painful honesty, she said, 'Because, apart from sex, you and I have nothing in common. I wouldn't fit into your world. You want me now, and that's f-fine—' she swallowed at the flare of anger in his eyes '—but you'll get tired of me eventually.'

'Tired of you?' His laugh was short and mirthless. 'I find you a constant surprise. Damn it, Giselle, I love you.'

'You don't know me,' she said, steeling her heart because he'd never know how much she'd cherish his words.

'Of course I know you, and I'm eager to find out more,' he said, his tone hard and aggressive. 'Tell me something, Giselle. Why did I leave you after only three days at

Flying Fish when I discovered that Parirua was once again
on the market?'

White-lipped and taut, she retorted, 'You've already
told me—because you wanted to buy Parirua and you don't
mix business and pleasure, and buying Parirua was business.' She finished on an angry half-sob, 'Because you're
an honourable man.'

'Partly that is true. I also suspected that when you found
out I'd bought Parirua you'd accuse me of using the desire
we both felt to manipulate you. And I was right—you did
think that.'

She muttered, 'I—yes. I'm sorry.'

'I didn't want our relationship clouded by such side
issues. And surely you must have known that our
meeting in Auckland wasn't a coincidence. I was there
because I needed to know that you were all right.' He
stopped, then went on brusquely, 'I didn't intend to make
love to you then. I wanted to take the six months of your
contract to woo you, but the moment I saw you again,
my defences crumbled. We had that night—and then
you left me.'

The repressed intensity in his words broke through the
shield of ice she'd surrounded herself with. Giselle's heart
slowed, then picked up speed. Without meeting his eyes
she confessed, 'Bella Adams came to tell me that she'd
seen us together in Paris. She was utterly convinced it was
me with you—that I'd changed my hair colour. I realised
she'd mistaken me for Leola. I—couldn't stay.'

She looked up into eyes that were narrowed and
intent—and furious. Her heart jumped, then contracted
into a tight ball.

But when he spoke it was in a calm, almost judicial tone.
'I still can't believe that you'd ever think that of me. But

when I realised just how little you value yourself against your sister, it began to make sense in an illogical way.'

'I was being illogical,' she admitted quietly. 'I could have asked Leola, but I couldn't bear to. I used that horrible suspicion as armour against you because I—because I…'

'Is it so hard to say, my dearest love?' he said with a smile that held tenderness and a wry amusement. 'You told me once you didn't believe in love at first sight; I agreed. Then you gave me your virginity. A woman who has lived until she is twenty-four before making love has to have a reason.'

He was getting perilously close to the truth. She said desperately, 'I didn't have the opportunity.'

'There are no young men within twenty kilometres of Parirua?' he said with tender mockery. 'Of course you had chances. Why did you choose me?'

She swallowed to ease her dry mouth. 'Because you're a prince,' she said roughly. 'A novelty.'

Roman laughed, a humourless sound that somehow added to the tension. 'I already know you well enough to be sure you don't give a hoot for the trappings of royalty. Why did you suggest we sleep together, Giselle?'

Thinly she said, 'Because I…because you're very sexy.'

He came towards her in two swift strides, stopping her retreat with just one finger under her chin, lifting it so that she was staring into his eyes. Her heart jolted in her chest, then began to race.

His voice harsh and completely determined, he said, 'Tell me the truth.'

'Damn you,' she whispered. 'What do you want—my heart's blood?'

'Yes,' he said simply. 'I want from you what I feel for you—'

'Passion isn't enough,' she cried.

'I know that. Oh, at first I thought that was all it was.' His voice deepened. 'I wanted you, yes, the second I saw you, but after a few days there was so much more than that.'

He closed his eyes for a moment, his hand dropping to his side. 'I want to find out what makes you tick behind that challenging face, to make you realise that you have so much to offer—and not only in bed, where you are a generous, passionate lover.'

Giselle began to speak, but the words died in her throat when he put his finger across her lips. She stared into the heart of a blue storm, searching for the truth, and saw it in his dark gaze, heard it in the hard, almost desperate tone of his voice.

'Hear me out. If this overwhelming hunger for you, this passionate need to protect you and make love to you and make you happy, this constant joy in your presence—if this is not love, Giselle, I don't know what it is. If you continue to say no, I will accept from you whatever you can give, and in time I will wear you down to accepting me as a husband. If not—' he held her gaze, his own keen and penetrating '—if you still will not marry me, my sweet love, I will come and live with you here and my brother can take over the care of the Sea Isles.'

'That's not fair,' she said, so moved she could barely summon any anger.

'Nico would certainly agree with you in that,' Roman said cheerfully.

'You're forcing me to make you choose—oh, can't you see? I don't know anything about being royal or—or rich, or giving dinner parties or receptions or anything. I'd be useless as a princess.'

'You are a farmer,' he said calmly. 'The Sea Isles need

someone to take an interest in what's left of their agriculture. And since you're intelligent and quick-witted, you'll soon learn how to conduct yourself. And you will always have me.'

When she hesitated, he asked, 'Do you love me?'

'Of course I love you,' she said indignantly, eyes glittering green in her pale face. 'That's not fair!'

'All is fair in love and war,' he quoted, smiling then added with such superb confidence that he almost convinced her, 'My dearest heart, together we can deal with anything.'

Tears blurred her eyes. In a shaken voice she said, 'I kept telling myself it was just the sex, but I always knew, deep down, that I was refusing to face the truth. I love you desperately—but I'm not the sort of woman you need in your life. I'll bet you've never even been in a supermarket.'

He stared at her as though she were mad, then flung his head back and laughed, a deep belly laugh that brought a reluctant smile to her lips. 'Then you'd be wrong. I bought food in supermarkets when I was at university.'

She knew she shouldn't ask, but it had been nagging at her for months, it seemed. 'And what about Bella Adams? I know she's left her husband and been seen around with you a lot—'

'Stop right there. You should have worked that out by now—it is quite easy to photograph two people together when they attend the same events and make sure a photographer is there to record the very brief meetings.'

She looked at him, her gaze questioning, and met eyes that were steady and darkly blue.

'I've been an utter idiot,' she admitted with another wry, half-formed smile.

His hands came out and gripped her shoulders. He even gave her a small shake before groaning and catching her close to him.

'You are everything I want,' he said, kissing the words onto her lips. 'Everything. I wish I could give you the reassurance you so obviously need, but I imagine it will take at least fifty years of long and happy marriage to do that, especially as we are going to have to live for some time in an ancient castle with at least two ghosts and some very primitive plumbing. I can hardly wait.'

Incredulously she looked up, and the fears that dammed her surrender gave way in a rush of hope and joy and complete trust. It seemed that one way or another she was going to have Roman for her husband. If he thought she could learn how to be a princess, she'd do it for him.

In a trembling voice she said, 'You told me that your cousin's wife was going to redecorate. Surely that covers the plumbing too? I can cope with ghosts, but the thought of very primitive plumbing makes my blood run cold.'

His mouth curving, he picked her up. 'Then that will be the first thing to be seen to. Direct me to your bedroom.'

Giselle turned her face into his throat, inhaling his particular scent—warm, infinitely familiar and reassuring. 'Are you going to use sex to persuade me?'

'Yes.'

'You probably should have tried that first,' she said demurely. 'It would have saved a lot of time. But just so you know, I'll marry you and live with you—I'll even try to be a princess—because I love you. I will always love you.'

He kissed her in a very satisfactory manner, then put her away from him, saying in a rough, impeded voice, 'Witch! You make me forget everything! Will you please show me where your bedroom is?'

Laughing, she took his hand and led him down the hall.

Much later, lying naked in his arms, she smiled at him, her heart swelling with a joy so direct and keen it was near to pain, and murmured, 'I'll ring Leola and tell her to start designing a wedding dress.'

'But not just now.' He slid a hand up to cup a breast, his thumb teasing the peak in an erotic movement that made her gasp.

'Not now,' she agreed, shivering at the honeyed tide of languorous hunger his touch summoned. 'She'll know I'm fine.'

'How?'

Giselle looked into his beloved face, the dominant features relaxed as she'd never seen them before, his heavy lashes half covering eyes that lazily scanned her face before moving to the soft curves of her breasts. He looked satisfied, she thought exultantly, sprawled on her bed like some great cat.

The scent of their lovemaking teased her nostrils; she turned her head and kissed the swell of one shoulder, then nipped it gently, relishing the swift hardening of the muscle at the tiny, provocative caress.

While she could still think, she tried to explain. 'There's a link—we always know how the other one is feeling. It's one of the reasons I was so sure that you had—that, well, you know. She was unhappy whenever I mentioned your name.'

'Perhaps she was afraid I would hurt you. Or sorry she'd mentioned Parirua. Or even sad because she was no longer with my brother,' he suggested.

She gave a little wriggle and heard his heartbeat pick up speed. Sighing, she kissed his jaw. 'I'm not going to ask her. And it's not weird or spooky or anything, it's just a twin thing.'

'I think you're asking me if I'll be jealous,' he said, confusing her with his astuteness. 'I shan't be, my dearest girl. I have been intensely jealous of Parirua, but not of your sister. There is room in our lives for her, just as I hope you will like my brother and my cousins. I know how reluctantly you loved me, and how difficult you think you will find it to be my wife and live in the public eye, but for much of the time we can be alone, and I think you will enjoy carrying out our responsibility to the islanders.'

He lifted her against his hardening body. 'We are noted for our long and satisfying marriages, we Magnati. I intend to spend the rest of my life making you, and our children, very happy indeed. And being with you will fill me with joy.'

He kissed her with growing passion, and she surrendered. There would be moments when she'd resent the many demands their life would make on them, but with Roman by her side she'd cope with anything, she thought dreamily, before letting him sweep her into the happiness of their future together.